MEET THE FORTUNES

Fortune (?) of the Month: Wesley "Wes" Robinson. Aka Wes Fortune?

Age: 33—and just a few minutes younger than his twin brother, which still irks him.

Vital statistics: Six feet plus with dark hair you'd love to rumple, laser-blue eyes, and don't forget that sexy *brain*.

Claim to Fame: Wes is the computer genius behind most of Robinson Tech's success.

Romantic prospects: Mr. Tall, Dark and Gorgeous believes "love" is nothing more than a chemical reaction. He thinks compatibility is a crock.

"I don't believe Vivian's new app can possibly work. Finding your perfect match via smartphone?

"However, I know a moneymaker when I see one. That's why I'm spending so much time conferring with Vivian. It's all about getting the product off the ground. And possibly proving my star developer wrong. It has nothing at all to do with her hazel eyes...or her persistent personality...or the way she gets me to reveal things I'd rather keep buried inside. I've heard enough of my father's Fortune history to know that wishing for a lifetime love is simply a pipe dream. Or is it?"

THE FORTUNES OF TEXAS:
ALL FORTUNE'S CHILDREN—
Money. Family. Cowboys.
Meet the Austin Fortunes!

Dear Reader,

What does computer programmer Vivian Blair know about love and romance? Well, she believes she knows enough to create a dating app that will find all frustrated, lonely singles a perfect partner. And her matching system has nothing to do with red-hot chemistry or flaming passion. She's convinced that compatibility is the only thing that will hold two people together.

Wes Robinson, vice president of research and development at Robinson Tech, is more than willing to pitch Vivian's dating app to the public. From a businessman's point of view, he's certain there are plenty of gullible, love-starved people who'll pay money to use My Perfect Match. But he's convinced the whole concept will eventually fail. As far as he's concerned, compatibility has nothing to do with love. It's all about desire and the spark that keeps it burning.

Vivian and Wes each set out to prove the other wrong and in the process both learn that the key to a lasting relationship is far more than lust or simply sharing the same interests. I hope you'll take the journey with Vivian and Wes as they discover the real meaning of love. And I hope each of you get to spend this Valentine's Day with the special love of your life.

Warmest wishes,

Stella

Fortune's Perfect Valentine

Stella Bagwell

HARLEQUIN® SPECIAL EDITION®

Special thanks and acknowledgment to Stella Bagwell for her contribution to the Fortunes of Texas: All Fortune's Children continuity.

Recycling programs
for this product may
not exist in your area

ISBN-13: 978-0-373-65937-1

Fortune's Perfect Valentine

Printed in U.S.A.

www.Harlequin.com

After writing more than eighty books for Harlequin, **Stella Bagwell** still finds it exciting to create new stories and bring her characters to life. She loves all things Western and has been married to her own real cowboy for forty-four years. Living on the south Texas coast, she also enjoys being outdoors and helping her husband care for the horses, cats and dog that call their small ranch home. The couple has one son, who teaches high school mathematics and is also an athletic director. Stella loves hearing from readers. They can contact her at stellabagwell@gmail.com.

Books by Stella Bagwell

Harlequin Special Edition

Men of the West

Christmas on the Silver Horn Ranch
Daddy Wore Spurs
The Lawman's Noelle
Wearing the Rancher's Ring
One Tall, Dusty Cowboy
A Daddy for Dillon
The Baby Truth
The Doctor's Calling
His Texas Baby
Christmas with the Mustang Man
His Medicine Woman
Daddy's Double Duty
His Texas Wildflower
The Deputy's Lost and Found
Branded with his Baby
Lone Star Daddy

Montana Mavericks: Striking It Rich

Paging Dr. Right

The Fortunes of Texas

The Heiress and the Sheriff

Visit the Author Profile page
at Harlequin.com for more titles.

To my husband, Harrell, and son, Jason.
With love to my two Valentines.

Chapter One

"So this little square picture of a key opening a heart is going to change the dating habits of the entire nation. I tap it with my fingertip and magically it will lead me to my true love." With a mocking snort, Wesley Robinson pushed the smartphone aside. "What a crock of crap."

Vivian Blair scowled at the man sitting behind the wide mahogany desk. At this moment, it didn't matter that he was her boss, who also happened to be Vice President of Research and Development at Robinson Tech. Nor did it matter that he happened to be the sexiest man she'd ever laid eyes on. This project was her baby and she had no intentions of letting him make a mockery of her hard work.

"I beg your pardon?" she asked, her voice rising along with her irritation. "This little button you're calling a crock of crap just happens to be a product of your company. A company owned and operated by your family, I might add. Have you forgotten that you approved this idea months ago?"

Ignoring her outburst, he calmly answered, "I've not forgotten anything, Vivian."

Throughout the six years she'd worked for Wes Robinson, he'd rarely called her by her given name, and on each occasion it had never failed to rattle her senses. Her boss was always strictly business. So having her name roll off his tongue was the closest he ever got to acknowledging she was a flesh-and-blood woman.

Vivian shifted on the edge of the wingback chair and did her best to refocus her jolted thoughts on their debate. "Then why are you so intent on degrading the product? I thought you were convinced it was going to make the company a pile of money."

With confident ease, he leaned back in the oxblood leather chair. After slipping a pair of tortoise-framed glasses from his nose, he leveled a somewhat smug gaze on her face. Vivian had the very unprofessional urge to stick her tongue out at him.

"I still believe the app is going to make money. And probably lots of it," he agreed. "But that doesn't mean I believe the theory behind the dating site will hold up. In fact, I'm willing to bet that after a few months the app's popularity will sink, simply because the public is going to realize that My Perfect Match won't fulfill its promise. Still, I'm willing to gamble the initial sales of the app will outweigh its short lifespan."

It was hard enough for Vivian to deal with having his eyes sliding leisurely over her face, but hearing him discount her hard work was even worse.

Leaning forward, she said briskly, "Forgive my bluntness, Mr. Robinson, but you're wrong. Completely wrong. My Perfect Match will work. My scientific research assures me that compatibility is the key to finding a perfect mate. The app will lead the consumer to a list of questions that follows strict criteria of the most important issues and topics in a person's private life. If they're answered truthfully, the computer will be able to match you with the perfect person based on corresponding answers."

His short laugh was weighted with sarcasm. "Sorry, but you just spouted a bunch of hooey. When a man sidles up to a woman at the bar, you think he has a list of questions on his mind?" Not waiting for her to answer, he plowed on, "There's only one question on his mind. And that's whether she'll say yes or no. He doesn't give a damn whether she eats fish twice a week, walks a mile a day or has a cat for a pet."

Vivian's back teeth clamped together as she fought to hold on to her dignity and her temper. "I might remind you that this app isn't an instrument for locating a one-night stand!" She tapped the screen of her phone. "This is a social aid to help lonely people find a perfect partner—one to spend the rest of their lives with happily. Or have you heard of that concept before?"

A wry expression crossed his face, and Vivian allowed her gaze to take a slow survey of his rugged features. At thirty-three years old, he was definitely coming into his prime, she decided. Piercing blue eyes sat beneath an unyielding line of dark brows, while a wide nose led down to a set of thin, chiseled lips. She couldn't remember a time she'd seen his strong, angled jaw without a dark shadow of day-old stubble or his short, coffee-brown hair in a style other than rumpled disarray. Yet she had to admit it was that touch of edginess that often pushed her thoughts in a naughty direction.

Many of Vivian's coworkers at Robinson Tech had trouble telling Wes apart from his identical twin, Ben, who was the newly appointed COO of the company. But Vivian could truthfully say she never got the two men mixed up. Unlike his brother Ben, Wes was rarely ever spotted in a suit and tie. Instead he usually arrived each morning for work in khakis or jeans. Yet it wasn't exactly their fashion choices that set the two men apart. Wes's quiet, reserved manner was totally opposite his brash twin's demeanor.

Clearly bored, he said, "I suppose you're talking about marriage now. I've heard enough on that subject this past month to last me a lifetime."

Since his brother Ben's wedding was taking place in about two weeks, on Valentine's Day, Vivian could only assume he was referring to that marriage. As far as she knew, Wes had never had a long-term girlfriend, much less been engaged. But then, she hardly knew what the man did outside this massive office building. She was only an employee, one of many who worked for the Robinson family.

Moving her gaze to a point just over his shoulder, she studied the skyline of downtown Austin. The capital of Texas had always been her home, yet she doubted that beyond this building, her footsteps had ever crossed Wes's path. Or, for that matter, the path of any other member of his wealthy family. That was just one of the reasons she never allowed herself to look at him as anything more than a boss, rather than a man with enough sex appeal to make a woman swoon.

Giving herself a hard mental shake, she countered his

statement with a question. "What else? If a person finds their perfect mate, the natural progression is marriage."

Vivian's gaze slipped back to his face just in time to see the corners of his mouth turn downward, and she realized this conversation was giving her more peeks into the man's private feelings than she'd ever expected to see. But then she'd never planned for this meeting to turn into a debate about dating or love or sex. Vivian hardly discussed such things with any man, much less her boss. *Awkward* couldn't begin to describe the turmoil she was feeling.

"Marriage is hardly the reason consumers will purchase the app," he said wryly. "But regardless of their motives, the concept won't work. The connection between a man and a woman is all about chemistry. It's the sparks—the fire—that fuse two people together. Not whether their likes and dislikes are the same."

Sparks? Fire? Maybe it would be nice to have a man take her into his arms and set a torch to her senses. But that sort of mindless passion didn't last. She had only to look at her own parents to see what happened between a man and a woman once the heat died and reality set in. Her mother had struggled to raise three children while her father had moved on to a younger woman. Now her mother lived alone, too disenchanted even to try to find a man to love her.

"Maybe attraction does initially pull two people together, but it hardly keeps them together," she argued. "And that's the problem My Perfect Match will fix. That's why it's going to be a huge success. Lasting relationships will eventually prove our product works."

The faint smile on his face was etched with amusement and was far too patronizing for her taste.

"I admire your enthusiasm, Ms. Blair."

He clearly didn't agree with her, and that notion bothered her far more than it should have. Vivian understood that this project had nothing to do with personal viewpoints. It was about producing a product that would ultimately make money for the company. Still, hearing his jaded ideas on the subject of relationships between men and women was maddening to her.

"But you think I'm wrong," she ventured. "If you're so sure this concept is going to be a bust, then why did you agree to it in the first place? In two weeks, on Valentine's Day, the app is scheduled to make its grand debut to the public. Don't you think it's rather late in the day to consider axing it?"

He cocked a brow at her. "What gave you the idea I want to ax it? Just because I don't believe in the concept? Look, Ms. Blair, I'm a businessman first and foremost, and I happen to believe consumers are just gullible enough to fall for this sort of baloney. As far as I'm concerned, whether it works or not is a moot point."

Wes watched as Vivian Blair's spine stiffened and her fingers fluttered to the top button of her crisp white shirt. Clearly he'd flustered the woman, which surprised him somewhat. He'd never seen her any way but cool and professional. During her six years as one of a team of computer developers employed by Robinson Tech, she'd proved herself to be dedicated, innovative and smart. She'd never failed to impress him with her work, but as a woman, she'd never really drawn a second look from him. Until this morning, when she'd snatched off her black-rimmed glasses and glared at him.

Her hazel eyes had thrown heated daggers straight at him, and her fiery reaction had caught him by complete surprise. All at once, he'd forgotten she was an employee. Instead, his mind had taken a momentary detour from work and started a subtle survey of her appearance.

He'd never thought of Vivian Blair as anything more than a coworker, a brainy, no-nonsense developer. She dressed neatly but primly in blouses and skirts that covered her slender frame with enough fabric to make even the strictest father nod with approval. What little jewelry she wore usually amounted to no more than a modest string of pearls or a fine gold chain and cross. Her pumps were low-heeled and pedestrian. And though her brown, honey-streaked hair was shiny and long enough to brush her shoulders, she rarely wore it loose. Instead she favored pulling it back into a bun or some sort of conservative twist.

No. Vivian Blair's appearance wasn't one that caught a man's attention. But seeing all that life sparking in her eyes had shown Wes a different side of her. And now, as her wide, full lips pressed into a tight line, he could only wonder what it might feel like to press his mouth to hers, to make those hard, cherry-colored lips yield softly to his.

Leaning slightly forward, he rested his forearms on the desktop and forced her gaze to meet his.

"Do you have a problem with that?" he asked.

If possible, the line of her lips grew even tighter, while her nostrils flared with disdain.

"Why should I?" she countered stiffly. "Your job is to make money. Mine is to create products. With My Perfect Match, we've both succeeded. Or, at least, we will succeed once the app goes on the market."

She was obviously trying to get her emotions under control, and for a moment Wes considered shooting a remark at her that would stir her temper all over again.

It would be fun to see, he thought. But she wasn't in his office for fun, and he hardly had time for it. Not with his twin brother, the COO of Robinson Tech, expecting Wes to put some new innovative idea on his desk every other day.

"You're on track now, Ms. Blair."

Her expression rigid, she reached for the small notepad and pen she'd placed on the edge of the desk when she'd first sat down for their meeting.

"So is the live remote still on for tomorrow?" she asked.

"I've already spoken with the producer of *Hey, USA* this morning. Our segment is set to be broadcast at nine fifteen central tomorrow. So I expect you to be ready well before that time."

She nodded. "And where do they plan to shoot this remote? The conference room?"

Wes shook his head. "Right here in my office." He jerked his thumb toward the window behind him. "We'll sit in front of the plate glass so the backdrop will be the skyline of the city. I think the producer—she wants an urban feel to the segment. You know, the image of city people hurrying and scurrying—too busy to find a date, so they rely on an app to find them one," he added drily.

"My Perfect Match is more than finding a person a date. It's—"

He held up a hand before she could slip into another sermon about compatibility and long-term relationships. Wes didn't want anything long-term. And he sure as hell wasn't looking to make any woman his wife. He'd seen his mother suffer through too many years of a loveless marriage to want the same for himself.

"Save it for the camera tomorrow," he told her. "The public is who you need to convince, not me."

She clutched the notebook to her chest, and Wes found himself wondering if she'd ever held a man to herself in that manner. He couldn't imagine it. But then, he didn't have a clue about her social life. Could be that once she was away from the Robinson Tech building, she tore off her professional demeanor and turned into a little wildcat. The idea very nearly put a smile on his face.

"Do you have any idea what sort of questions the interviewer will be asking? I'd like to be prepared."

"You've had plenty to say on the subject during our meeting this morning," he told her. "And I'm sure you won't have any problem speaking your mind tomorrow. You'll simply explain the product and how it works. I'll speak for Robinson Tech and what the company stands for. The national exposure will be great."

She dropped the notepad to her lap, but Wes's gaze lingered on the subtle curves of her breasts beneath the white shirt. Damn it, what was wrong with him? He didn't need to be ogling this woman. There were always plenty of women in his little black book who were ready to go out on a date with him. He certainly didn't need to start having romantic notions about Vivian.

"Yes, the publicity is just what the app needs," she said primly. "I only hope everything goes smoothly."

Annoyed at his straying thoughts, he frowned at her. "Why should it not?"

Clearing her throat, she said, "I've never been on television before."

He leveled a pointed look at her. "I'm sure there are plenty of things you've never done before, Ms. Blair. And there's always a first time for everything."

She straightened her shoulders, and once again Wes spotted a flash of anger in her eyes.

"You're very reassuring," she said.

"I'm not your caretaker, Ms. Blair."

"Thank God."

The words were muttered so quietly that at first Wes wasn't sure he heard them. And once he'd concluded he'd heard correctly, he couldn't quite believe she'd had the audacity to say them.

"What did you say?" he demanded.

Louder now, she answered, "I said, are we finished here?"

Any other time he would've upbraided an employee for making such a retort, but seeing Vivian Blair turn into a firecracker right in front of his eyes had knocked him off kilter.

"Yes. Be here in my office no later than eight forty-five in the morning. I don't want any glitches or mishaps happening before the interview."

"I'll certainly be on time."

She quickly rose to her feet and started toward the door. Before Wes could stop himself, he added, "And Ms. Blair, tomorrow for the interview, could you not look so—studious? My Perfect Match is all about romance. It might help if you—well, looked the part a bit more."

Her back went ramrod straight as she fixed him with a stare. "In other words, sex sells," she retorted. "Is that what you're trying to tell me?"

To a woman like Vivian, he supposed he sounded crude. But she should have understood that this was all about business. Still, something about the disdain on her face caused a wave of heat to wash up his neck and over his jaw. He could only hope the overhead lighting was too dim for her to pick up his discomfort.

Clearing his throat, he purposely swiveled his chair

so that he was facing her. He'd be damned if he let this woman make him feel the least bit ashamed.

"Ms. Blair, there's no cause for you to be offended. I'm not trying to exploit you or your gender. I'm trying to sell an idea. Having you look attractive and pretty can only help the matter."

Even from the distance of a few feet, he could see her heave out a long breath. For one split second he was so tempted to see that fire in her eyes again that he almost left his chair and walked over to her. But he forced himself to stay put and behave as her boss, instead of a hot-blooded male.

Tilting her little chin to a challenging angle, she asked brusquely, "And what about your effort in all of this, Mr. Robinson? Do you plan to wax your chest and unbutton your shirt down to your waist?"

It took Wes a moment to digest her questions, but once they sank in, his reaction was to burst out laughing.

"Touché, Vivian. I expect I deserved that."

"I expect you did," she said flatly, then turned and left the room.

As Wes watched the door close behind her, he realized this was the first time in days that he'd laughed about anything. Strange, he thought, that a brainy employee had been the one to put a smile on his face.

Shaking his head with wry disbelief, he turned his chair back to the desk and reached for a stack of reports.

By the time Vivian returned to her work cubicle, she felt certain that steam was shooting from her ears. Before today, she'd never allowed herself to think of Wes Robinson as anything other than her boss. She'd kept herself immune to his dark good looks. A rather easy task, given the fact that he was so far out of her league, she needed a telescope to see him. But their meeting this morning had definitely given her a full view of the man. And what she'd seen she certainly disliked.

"Hey, Viv, ready for lunch?"

Pressing fingertips to the middle of her puckered forehead, she looked over her shoulder to see George Townsend standing at the entrance of her work cubicle. In his early fifties, he was a tall, burly man with red hair and a thick beard to match. Other than a set of elderly parents who lived more than a thousand miles away, he had no family. Instead, he seemed content to let his work be his family. Most everyone in the developmental department considered George a social recluse. Except Vivian.

During the years they'd worked together, she'd grown close to George. Now she considered him as much of a brother as she did a coworker. And she was thankful for their friendship. In her opinion, the man was not only a computer genius but also a kind human being. He didn't care about her appearance. Nor was he interested in the size of her apartment or bank account.

"Is it that time already? I'm not really hungry yet." Actually, the way she felt at the moment, she didn't think she'd be able to stomach any kind of food for the remainder of the day. Thoughts of Wes Robinson's smart-mouthed remarks were still making her blood boil.

"It's nearly twelve," he said with a frown, then added temptingly, "and I brought enough dewberry cobbler for the both of us, too."

Sighing, she put down her pencil and rose to her feet. For George's sake, she'd do her best to have lunch and try to appear normal.

"Okay," she told him. "Let me log out and we'll go."

Once she left her desk, the two of them walked through the work area until they reached a fair-sized break room equipped with a row of cabinets, refrigerator, microwave, hot plate and coffee machine.

Even though it was lunchtime, only a handful of people were sitting at the long utility tables. Since Robinson Tech was located in downtown Austin, most of the employees who worked in Vivian's department went out to lunch. There were several good eating places within walking distance and they all strived to give quick service to the workers on a limited time schedule. But usually Vivian chose to bring her own lunch and remain in the building.

"Looks like most of your friends are out today," George said as the two of them took seats across from each other. "Guess they don't mind walking in the cold."

Vivian didn't mind the cold, either. But she did mind sitting at a table with a group of giggling women with little more on their minds than the latest hairdo, a nail salon or a man.

"The wind was very cold this morning," she agreed. "I was already here at the building before the heater in my car ever got warm."

As she'd readied herself for work this morning, she'd also dressed more warmly in dark gray slacks and dress boots. The gray cardigan she'd pulled over her white shirt had looked perfectly appropriate to her, but now, as she glanced down at herself, she was doubting her fashion choices.

Damn Wes Robinson! What did he know about women and sex and romance, anyway?

Probably a whole lot more than you do, Vivian. It's been weeks since you've been on a date, and that eve-

*ning turned out to be as exciting as watching a cater-
pillar slowly climb a blade of green grass.*

"Well, Mr. Robinson's office must have been plenty
warm," George commented between bites of sandwich.
"You looked pretty hot when you got back to your desk."

Vivian shot her friend an annoyed look. "You noticed?"

He smiled. "I just happened to look up. Did anything
go wrong with the meeting?"

She let out a heavy breath. "I just don't agree with
some of the man's ideas, that's all. And frankly, I'll
be glad when the introduction of My Perfect Match is
over and done with. I'm a computer developer, George.
I don't work in advertising."

"But you are going to do the TV spot in the morning, aren't you?"

The smirk on her face revealed exactly how she felt
about being on a national television show that pulled in
millions of viewers each morning. "I have no choice.
Wes—I mean, Mr. Robinson—wants me to explain how
the app works."

"Well, it is your brainchild," George reasoned.

Reaching across the table, she gave his hand a
friendly pat. "I could've never created the app without
your help, George. You're the wizard here. As far as
I'm concerned, you can explain how the thing works
far better than I."

He chuckled. "Only the technical parts. All those
questions and what they're supposed to do for the person answering them—well, that's more your line."

Vivian had stood in line for nearly ten minutes this
morning at Garcia's Deli just to get one of Mr. Garcia's
delicious pork sandwiches called the Cuban Cigar, but

now each bite she took seemed to stick at the top of her throat.

Shaking her head, she said, "Not really. Those questions were compiled by a set of psychologists who are experts in human relationships. But I do believe in them. And you should, too, George. Otherwise, our little brainchild will be a bust."

And after the way she'd defended the new app to her cynical boss, seeing it fall flat would just about kill her.

He shrugged one thick shoulder. "I'm not worried. We've developed some stinkers before and survived. Not everything we create is going to be a huge success."

No. In this age of fast-moving technology, it was hard to predict what the public would spend its hard-earned money on. Yet Vivian knew first-hand that being lonely was a painful thing. Her many failures at finding true love were the main reason she'd come up with My Perfect Match. At the age of twenty-eight, she would be silly to consider herself an old maid, yet she was growing tired of playing the dating game and falling short of having any sort of meaningful relationship to show for it. Her own frustration led her to believe there were plenty of lonely people out there who'd be willing to give the app a try.

"That's true. But I've really stuck my neck on the chopping block for this project. More than anything, I want it to be a huge success. That's why I can't falter in the interview tomorrow."

George's coarse, ruddy features spread into a reassuring smile. "Don't think about your nerves. Just look into the camera and pretend you're talking to me. You'll be great."

Great? Sitting in front of a television camera with Wes Robinson at her side? She'd count herself lucky to simply hold herself together.

Chapter Two

Back in Wes's office, he was just hanging up the phone with the marketing department when his twin brother, Ben, walked through the door.

"Looks like I need to have a long talk with my secretary." He leaned back in the desk chair and folded his arms across his chest. "Normally, Adelle knows better than to let riffraff come into my office unannounced."

Clearly amused by his brother's sardonic jab, Ben walked over and rested the corner of his hip on Wes's desk. Dressed in a dapper gray suit and burgundy patterned tie, Ben was every inch the business man and more like their father than Wes would ever want to be. Full of brass and swagger, Ben went after anything and everything he wanted with the ferocity of a stalking tiger.

For a while after their father, Gerald, had appointed Ben the new COO of Robinson Tech, Wes had felt worse than slighted. He'd been cut to the core. As vice president of the developmental team, Wes was adept at presiding over operations, generating revenue, analyzing financial reports and motivating staff, along with a jillion other responsibilities that went along with the job. He could've handled the COO position with his eyes closed.

But Gerald had chosen to hand it to his elder twin. And to Wes the reason had been blatantly obvious. Because Ben was their father's favorite. Which wasn't hard to understand, given the fact that Ben had the same aggressive business tactics as their father, while Wes considered hard work and integrity the best way to climb the corporate ladder.

Grinning, Ben said, "I'm glad to see you're getting your wit back."

"I wasn't aware I'd ever lost it," Wes quipped.

Ben thoughtfully picked up a paperweight and held it up to the florescent light. The hunk of gray glass was the shape of a dove, and Wes wondered if Ben was thinking the bird matched his younger twin. No doubt their father would say Wes was the peaceful dove of the two, while Ben was a fierce hawk. The idea stung far more than Wes wanted to admit.

"Hmm. Ever since I got the COO position, you've been about as warm as a polar bear. I thought you'd be over Dad's decision by now."

Wes inwardly bristled while trying to make sure his expression remained bland. No one could rankle him more than his twin, but he hardly wanted Ben to know that. The man was already smug enough.

"I was over it five minutes after Dad's decision was announced," Wes told him.

Ben's expression said he found Wes's statement

laughable. Which came as no surprise. From the years when they were small boys until now, the two of them had been rivals in everything, including their parents' love and admiration. And Wes supposed he'd spent most all of his thirty-three years trying to prove he was equal or better than his slightly older brother.

"If that's the case, then why have you been giving me the cold shoulder?"

"That's all in your mind," Wes told him.

Placing the dove back on the desk, Ben rose to his feet and walked over to the wall of plate glass. Wes watched as his brother stood in a wide stance, his hands linked at his back as he stared out at the city skyline.

"If it's not the COO position that's bothering you, then you're upset with me about my search for our Fortune heritage. I would've thought you'd want to know Keaton Whitfield is our half brother."

Wesley heaved out a weary breath. Crashing Kate Fortune's ninetieth birthday party and creating a scandalous scene had been bad enough. But Ben hadn't stopped there. He'd set out on a wild search to dig up hidden branches of the family tree, and in doing so, he'd already unearthed one of their father's illegitimate children.

"I don't have any complaints about Keaton—not personally. It's you and this dogged search you're making. Just for once I wish you'd stop and consider Mother's feelings in this matter. How do you think all of this makes her feel? Can you imagine the pain and humiliation she must feel to know that her husband cheated on her, not just once, but probably many times?"

"Damn it, Wes, I'm not on a quest to punish our mother. I want Dad's rightful place in the Fortune family to be reestablished. I want the Fortunes, especially Kate, to have to acknowledge the truth publicly."

Wes snorted. "The truth! Regarding our father, we don't know what the hell the truth might be. Dad is hiding things about his past. Rachel already figured out that much when she found some of Dad's old correspondence and the driver's license with his name listed as Jerome Fortune. But as far as I'm concerned, Dad can keep his secrets. I'm perfectly content with the number of siblings I have now. And I sure don't need the Fortune name tacked on to Robinson just to make me feel important."

With a shake of his head, Ben walked back over to Wes's desk, but this time he didn't take a seat. Instead, he stood, his hands jammed in the pockets of his trousers as he gazed down at his brother.

"We see everything about this Fortune thing differently. Wouldn't you like to know the truth about our father?"

Wes answered, "Not if the truth hurts."

Ben grimaced. "Did you ever think that restoring the integrity of our father's heritage might help mend some of the cracks in our family?"

Wes wanted to ask him how uncovering Gerald's true parentage could possibly mend years of their father's deceit, but he didn't bother. Instead, he said, "I'm not the only one against this quest of yours. Most of our siblings side with me on this thing. The Robinson family doesn't need the bad publicity that this expedition of yours might bring to our name and Dad's legacy in the business world." He leveled a challenging look at his twin. "In the end, Ben, what will we really gain?"

"The truth. Justice. Vindication. Take your pick. Although I doubt any of those reasons are enough to satisfy you."

Knowing he was wasting his time and effort on the Fortune family matter, Wes decided to move their conversation elsewhere. "I was about to go to lunch. Was there some reason you stopped by my office this morning? Other than to discuss Dad's hidden past?"

"Actually, I stopped by to ask you about the new app you're promoting for Valentine's Day. I hear you're getting television coverage."

"That's right. Tomorrow, in fact. A colleague and I will be doing a live remote for *Hey, USA* from here in my office."

"A national morning show? Impressive," Ben said, then grinned slyly. "I'm surprised you managed to garner their attention. You must be doing something right, little brother."

Even though physical wrestling matches with his twin had ended in their high school days, there were times Wes still got the playful urge to box his brother's jaw.

"Thanks, but in case you haven't noticed, we do have an excellent marketing department at Robinson Tech," Wes told him. "And given the fact that dating and love and all that sort of nonsense usually garner lots of attention, it wasn't hard for them to snare a segment on *Hey, USA*."

Ben shot his brother a patient smile. "Nonsense? Sorry, brother, but you have a lot to learn. Finding the right girl to love is what life is all about. When you meet finally meet her, you'll understand completely."

Wes couldn't imagine any woman making him want to step into the role of husband and father. Not with the example Gerald had set for his sons.

"There is no right girl," Wes told him. "Not for me.

But that doesn't mean I'm not happy for you. How are the wedding plans coming along?"

"Everything is on track, I think."

"I'm assuming the wedding is going to be a big affair," Wes stated the obvious. He'd already overheard his brother discussing an orchestra and enough bottles of expensive champagne to float a battleship.

"Ella deserves the very best. I've told her she can have anything she wants and I'm going to make sure she gets it." His features grew soft. "When you really love a woman, Wes, you want to give her the world. When the time comes, you'll understand that part of it, too."

Wes could understand his brother wanting to give his fiancée the best of everything. From what he understood, Ella was raised by a single mom in a household with very little money. To make matters worse, her younger brother had cerebral palsy and needed extra care. What did surprise Wes was the amount of love and affection he saw on Ben's face each time he spoke of his fiancée. Wes had never imagined his brother capable of such tender feelings. But somehow Ella had managed to bring out the gentle side of the tiger.

"I'm glad you want to make Ella happy. She does deserve it. But as for me, I'm content to let you be the married twin. I'm staying single."

"Never say never, brother," Ben warned. "When you stand up at the wedding as my best man, the love bug just might bite you."

"I'll be sure and wear plenty of bug spray underneath my tux," Wes replied.

Chuckling, Ben started toward the door. "I'm off to lunch. Good luck on tomorrow's remote. If I'm not in a meeting at that hour, I'll try to drop by and watch you in action."

"I'll do my best not to let the company down."

With his hand on the doorknob, Ben paused long enough to glance over his shoulder. "That's one thing I never worry about."

Wes might have lost the COO position to his twin, but he could never blame Ben for Gerald's decision. No matter the rivalry between the two of them, he and Ben had the special bond of love that most twins shared. As far as Wes was concerned, their bond might get a bit frazzled at times, but it would never be broken.

"Thanks, Ben."

Once his brother disappeared through the door, Wes left his desk and grabbed a heavy jacket from a small closet. Outside his office, he paused at his secretary's desk. At eighty years old, Adelle should have been gray and prune-faced. Instead, her red, perfectly coifed hair was merely threaded with gray and her smooth skin could have been a poster for the Fortune Youth Serum. Wes figured most women Adelle's age had given up working long ago. But Adelle showed very little sign of slowing down, much less heading for a rocking chair. Each day after work, she walked a mile, then stopped at her favorite bar for a gin and tonic.

At the moment, she was peering at him over the top of pink-framed reading glasses.

"I'm going down the street for lunch," he informed her. "Is there anything on my agenda before one thirty?"

She glanced at a spiral-bound notepad lying on the left side of the desk, and Wes inwardly shook his head. The woman worked for one of the most technically advanced computer companies in the world, but she chose to use paper and pencil. Wes overlooked Adelle's archaic work preferences, mainly because he liked her and couldn't imagine his life without her in it. And as a secretary, she was priceless. As far as he was concerned, he didn't care if she used a chisel and stone. All that mattered to him was that she always kept his office running smoothly.

"No. Nothing until two," she declared. "And that meeting is with Mort. I've cut you thirty minutes for him. Is that enough time?"

Mort Conley was a member of the same developmental team that included Vivian Blair. The young guy was a guru at creating computer commands, but he lacked the creative imagination to create an innovate product on his own, like Vivian had with My Perfect Match. Still, Wes respected his enthusiasm and had agreed to look at a new app design related to sports fans.

"Should be plenty," he answered. "And I'll be back before two."

Wes started to move away from the secretary's desk, but she stopped him with another question.

"What did you do to Ms. Blair? She stalked out of your office like she wanted to murder somebody."

It wasn't unusual for Adelle to speak her mind with Wes. After all, she'd been his secretary for many years, and over that time they'd grown close. Still, it surprised him that she'd taken that much notice of Vivian Blair.

"I didn't *do* anything to her. I simply told her to be prepared for the TV segment in the morning."

Clearly unconvinced, the woman smirked at him. "Before today I've never seen as much as a frown on Vivian's face. You must have said something mean—or threatened her in some way. What were you thinking? She's one of the brightest workers on the developmental team! Along with that, she's a sweet little soul who wouldn't swat a bee even if it was stinging her."

Vivian had hardly come off as a sweet little soul this

morning when he'd voiced his personal feelings about her computer-generated idea of dating, Wes thought. To Adelle he said, "I wasn't aware you knew Vivian so well."

His secretary let out an unladylike snort. "You don't have to have supper with a person every night to know her. Women have instincts about other women and plenty of other things. You ought to understand that, Mr. Robinson."

Considering the vast difference in their ages, it seemed ridiculous for Adelle to call him "Mr. Robinson," a fact he'd pointed out to her many times before. But she insisted that calling him Wes wouldn't appear professional, so he'd given up trying to change her.

"Ah, yes. Women and their instincts," he said drily. "They're always right. I'm sure your late husband never argued with you."

"Rudy always respected my opinion, God rest his soul. That's why we celebrated fifty-five years of marriage before he passed on. You need to remember to respect Vivian's opinion—whether you agree with it or not."

Wes stared at her. "Have you been pressing your ear against the door of my office?"

"I hardly need to," she retorted, then turned her attention back to the work on her desk.

As Wes made his way out of the Robinson Tech office building, he mentally shook his head. This morning, he'd heard all he wanted to hear about women and dating and love. Yet as he passed the area where Vivian Blair worked, he found himself wondering if she was still miffed at him. And wondering, too, if she ever went out to lunch with a man, or a romantic dinner in the evening.

While heading down the sidewalk to his favorite bar

and grill, Wes very nearly smiled at that last notion. He couldn't imagine Vivian Blair finding her perfect match in a dimly lit café with violin music playing sweetly in the background and soft candlelight flickering in her hazel eyes. No, she'd be looking for her perfect man in a stuffy computer lab.

The next morning before she left her apartment, Vivian gave her image one last glance in the mirror. Last night she'd agonized for hours over what to wear for the television segment. When Wes had suggested she not look so studious, her first instinct had been to go out and find a dress that showed plenty of cleavage and lots of leg, a pair of fishnet stockings and platform heels. If he wanted a ditzy bimbo to represent Robinson Tech, then she'd give him one. But in the end, she had too much pride to make such a fool of herself. She didn't need to show Wes she could be sexy. She needed to prove that a compatible mate was far more important than flaming-hot chemistry.

Stepping back from the cheval mirror, she adjusted the hem of the close-fitting black turtleneck, then smoothed her hands over the hips of the matching black slacks she'd chosen to wear. The garments weren't frilly or feminine, but their close-fitting cut revealed her slender curves. And her golden hoop earrings were far more daring than the pearl studs she normally wore to work.

Wes Robinson would be unhappy because she didn't look like a sex kitten, Vivian supposed. But she didn't care. She was hardly going to change her style or her viewpoint for him.

Some fifteen minutes later, she parked her car in the underground parking garage of Robinson Tech and rode the elevator up to the floor that housed the developmental team, along with Wes's office.

By the time she neared her work space, George was already there waiting for her to arrive.

Glancing at his watch, he said, "Damn, Vivian, I thought you were going to be late."

"I had a bad night and slept through the alarm," she explained. Actually, *bad night* was an understatement. She'd lain awake for hours, her thoughts vacillating between Wes's infuriating remarks and concerns about the television interview. When she'd applied her makeup, she'd tried her best to hide the circles of fatigue beneath her eyes. "Do I look okay? I mean, for television?"

He let out a low whistle, and Vivian laughed.

"Thanks, George, for your vote of confidence. I definitely need it this morning. My stomach is fluttering like it's full of angry bees."

"I'll go fetch you a cup of coffee with plenty of cream. That should help."

"No! Thank you, George. My nerves are already frazzled enough without a dose of caffeine." To be honest, she was about to jump out of her skin. The notion of being on national television was scary. Especially to someone who'd practically wilted into a faint when she'd been forced to give a salutatorian speech at her high school graduation ceremony. Yet if she was being honest with herself, she had to admit it was the thought of seeing Wes again that was really tying her stomach into knots. Which was ridiculous. She'd worked closely with the man for several years now.

Yes, but she'd never had an argument about love and sex and marriage with him before.

Turning to her desk, Vivian flipped on her computer and locked her handbag in the bottom drawer.

"Hey, Viv, good luck on the TV spot this morning. Are you ready to face the camera?"

Vivian looked around to see Justine, a fellow developer, standing next to George at the entrance of the cubicle. The petite young blonde wearing a short, chic hairdo and a tight pencil skirt was more Wes's style, Vivian couldn't help thinking.

"Thanks, Justine. I'm telling myself I'm ready whether I am or not. Actually, I wish you or George would take my place in this interview. I feel like I'm headed toward a firing squad."

Justine laughed. "George and I aren't camera-friendly. We're tech geeks, right, George?"

The burly man chuckled. "Right. But with you representing us, you can show everybody that it's our team that keeps this company in the black. Without our creations, they wouldn't have anything to sell. If My Perfect Match becomes a hit, we might actually get the recognition around here that we deserve."

"And a bonus to go with it," Justine added on a hopeful note.

"Oh, thanks, you two," Vivian said drily. "I really needed that added pressure right now."

George glanced at his watch. "You'd better head on to the boss's office," he warned. "You don't want to be late."

Already turning to leave, Justine said, "And I'm going to go tune in to *Hey, USA*. Do us proud, Viv."

Moments later, as Vivian headed to Wes's office, the word *proud* continued to waltz through her head. Yes, she had pride in her work as a developer and pride as a woman who had her own ideas of what made relationships work. This morning when the camera started rolling, she had to make sure she was strong, persuasive and full of conviction, even if Wes believed her ideas were a bunch of crap.

When she reached Adelle's desk, the secretary waved her onward. "I should warn you, it's a madhouse in there, Vivian. Don't let the chaos rattle you."

"I'll do my best," Vivian told her, while thinking it wasn't the broadcast crew she was concerned about; it was her irritating boss.

Resisting the urge to smooth her hair, Vivian opened the door to Wes's office and stepped inside. In that instant, she realized Adelle's warning was correct. The place was a jumbled mess of equipment and people. Behind Wes's desk, near the vast window overlooking the city, lights and cameras were being set up to garner the best angle. Cables and electrical wirings were being pulled here and there over the polished parquet, while, across the room, a makeup person was trying to brush powder across Wes's forehead.

"Get that stuff away from me," he ordered the diminutive blonde chasing after him with a long-handled makeup brush. "I don't care if my face shines."

"I'm sorry, Mr. Robinson, but the glare of the light—"

Before the harried woman could finish her plea, Wes quickly walked over to Vivian standing uncertainly in the middle of the room.

"Good morning, Ms. Blair. Are you ready for this?" He waved a hand to the commotion of the crew behind them.

She drew in a bracing breath, while trying to ignore the way his blue eyes were making a slow, deliberate search of her face. What was the man thinking? That she needed help from the makeup woman? The idea stung.

"I think so. I've been going over all the things I

need to say about My Perfect Match. I just hope the interviewer asks the right questions. Do you know what anchorperson will be doing our segment?"

"Ted Reynolds. I rarely watch television, so I'm not that familiar with the guy. Are you?"

Vivian rubbed her sweaty palms down the sides of her hips. "Yes. He's the darling of the network morning shows and the reason *Hey, USA* is such a hit."

"Great. The more star power, the better for us," Wes remarked, then suddenly wrapped his hand over her shoulder. "Are you okay, Vivian? You're looking very pale."

If she resembled a ghost, then the shock of his touch was taking care of the problem. Hot blood was shooting straight from his hand on her shoulder all the way to her face. He'd never touched her before. Not like this. Maybe their fingers had inadvertently brushed from time to time, but he'd never deliberately put his hand on her. Why had he suddenly decided to touch her today of all days?

Don't be stupid, Vivian. The man is simply steadying you because you look like a wilted noodle ready to fall at his feet. That's all it means. Nothing more.

"I'm fine," she muttered. "I just want this to be over with so I can get back to work."

She was trying to decide how to disengage her shoulder from his hand without appearing too obvious, when a member of the production crew spoke up.

"Mr. Robinson, it's nearly time to go on the air. We need you and Ms. Blair to take your seats and let us wire you with earpieces."

The thin young man with a shaved head, red goatee and skintight black jeans motioned to the two of them, prompting Vivian to ask, "Who is he?"

"A guy who wishes he was in Hollywood instead of Austin," Wes said drily, then added in a more serious tone, "actually, his is Antonio. He's the manager of this affiliate crew."

With his hand moving to the small of her back, Wes ushered her forward. "Come on. Let's go put on our act."

Act? Wes might be planning to put on an act for the camera. But Vivian was going to speak straight from the heart. Whether he liked it or not.

Chapter Three

Five minutes later, Wes and Vivian sat side by side in a pair of dark blue wingback chairs and stared at a monitor positioned in front of them, yet out of view of the camera lens.

A few steps to their left, Antonio stood at the ready, his finger pointed at the monitor. "Get ready," he instructed. "As soon as this commercial ends, Ted will greet you and introduce you to the viewing audience."

Vivian's heart was suddenly pounding so hard she could hardly hear herself think. As much as she wanted to duck behind the chair and hide from the camera, she had to remain at Wes's side and face the viewing audience.

Her hands laced tightly together upon her lap while her mouth felt as if she'd just eaten a handful of chalk. Just as she was trying to convince herself she wasn't going to panic, she felt a hand at the side of her face.

Turning slightly, she realized with a sense of shock

that the hand belonged to Wes and his fingers were gently tucking her hair behind her ear.

"So everyone can see your face better," he explained under his breath.

As if Vivian wasn't already shaken enough, the man had to start touching her like a familiar lover! The idea of being on television must be doing something to him, she thought.

Sucking in a deep breath, she resisted the urge to shake her hair loose so that it would drape against her cheek. "I think—"

Antonio suddenly interrupted her retort. "Here we go," he warned. "Three, two, one—you're on!"

Vivian straightened stiffly in her seat and stared dazedly at the television monitor, while inches away, Wes leaned comfortably back and, with an easy smile, gazed at the camera.

What a ham! During the years she'd been at Robinson Tech, she'd not heard of anyone in the company's developmental team or its vice president being on television. Yet he was behaving as though he did this sort of thing every day.

Just as she was thinking Wes ought to go into the acting profession, Ted Reynolds's image popped onto the screen. Dressed in a flamboyant, brick-red jacket and a blue patterned tie, he had subtly highlighted hair slicked back from his broad face. Through the earpiece she could hear his voice giving the two of them a routine greeting and introduction.

Once they'd responded to his welcoming words, Ted quickly slipped into the role of interviewer. When he asked Wes to give the audience an overview of the company, her boss smoothly went into a brief summary of what Robinson Tech was all about, and the huge strides it had made in recent years at providing the consumer with affordable, up-to-date technology for use in homes and offices.

While Wes was doing a flawless job at praising the company's capabilities and progress, Vivian was trying her hardest to remain focused on the words being exchanged between the two men. But she was rapidly losing the battle. Instead of following their conversation, her mind began drifting to the ridiculous. Like the tangy scent of expensive cologne wafting from Wes's white dress shirt. The way his dark hair lay in mussed waves and the shape of his long fingers resting against his thigh. On his right hand he wore a heavy ring set with onyx, but the left hand was bare. No, she thought wryly. Wes wouldn't be wearing a ring on his left. Not unless a perfect princess came along and swept him up in a cloud of bliss.

Stop it, Vivian! Get your mind back on track! Otherwise, you're going to be lost.

The words of warning going off in her head prompted her to give herself a hard mental shake and stare intensely at the monitor. Maybe if she kept her eyes on Ted Reynolds, she'd forget all about Wes's nearness.

The popular host continued, "In the past few years, Robinson Tech has given us some great products. The tablet for kids—when it first came on the market, my daughter was jumping up and down for it. And by the way, she loves it. Do you believe this new app will be as successful as some of the more popular items your company has produced in the past?"

Vivian looked over at Wes and wondered just how much acting this was going to require from her boss. Successful? She clamped her lips shut to prevent a nervous laugh from bursting out of her. Why didn't he be honest and tell Ted he thought it was a crock of crap? Just as he'd told her less than twenty-four hours ago?

An engaging grin brought the hint of a dimple in his left cheek, and Vivian had to stifle a groan. He'd certainly never shown this charming side of himself when she was around. In fact, she'd never dreamed he possessed an ounce of playfulness. Moment by moment, she was learning there were many facets of Wes that she'd never seen before. Or was this just all a part of his act? she wondered.

"I have a great amount of confidence in our new app. On the surface it might appear that My Perfect Match is designed for young people, but actually it's geared for all ages. After all, love has no age limit. Don't you agree?"

The host chuckled slyly. "I'd better agree, Wes. Otherwise, my wife will have me sleeping in the doghouse tonight."

Oh, please, Vivian wanted to shout. My Perfect Match was nothing to jest about.

She noticed Wes was chuckling along with Ted as though the two of them were sharing a private joke about the opposite sex. The idea stirred her temper as much as Wes's nearness was disturbing her senses.

Ted went on, "So you're telling me that all people interested in finding a mate, no matter their age, can get results using My Perfect Match?"

"I'm absolutely certain of it," Wes answered without hesitation.

The anchor appeared surprised at Wes's unwavering response, while Vivian was downright stunned. She'd expected him to give himself a little wiggle room, just in case the app did fail. Was this more of his pretense? If it was, then what else did he go around pretending?

"Wow, that's quite a statement," Ted responded. "Especially coming from the vice president of the company."

"Vice President of Research and Development," Wes corrected him.

"Uh, okay. Well, can you tell me how this is supposed to work?" A leering grin came over the man's face. "Say I'm a lonely guy looking for a woman to settle down with. How will the app help me?"

"It'll save you a big bar tab," Wes quipped, then softened his response with another charming grin. "Seriously, I think Vivian can better answer that question."

Vivian felt like a million eyes were suddenly focusing on her face. Her heart kicked into an even faster pace, sending a loud whooshing noise to her ears. She darted a glance at Wes, then froze a wide-eyed gaze on the monitor and Ted's smirking face.

"Good morning again, Vivian."

She desperately needed to clear the ball of nerves in her throat, but it was too late, so instead she swallowed. The effort practically strangled her, making her voice sound more like a squeak. "Good morning."

The show host gave her a wide, plastic smile and Vivian promised herself she'd never again tune in to *Hey, USA*.

"I hear you are the brains behind this new technical device to find love," he said. "Would you care to explain to our viewing audience exactly how the app works?"

Shifting slighting on the seat, she resisted the urge to swallow a second time. "Uh—yes, it matches you with the right people. I mean—right person."

"Could you elaborate a little?" Ted urged.

"Oh, well—it's the questions. And how you answer and—that sort of thing."

Oh, Lord, I'm making a mess of this, she thought frantically. She had to pull herself together before she made a complete idiot of herself!

"Okay, say I answer all the questions listed on the program," the interviewer went on. "Then what? A woman out there looking for her perfect man decides if she likes my answers? Isn't that the same premise of all the dating sites being advertised nowadays?"

"No—My Perfect Match is different. A woman won't decide if she likes you—the computer will do the deciding," Vivian attempted to correct him.

The popular television personality chuckled, and Vivian couldn't decide whether she wanted to crawl under her chair or throw her shoe straight through the monitor.

"I'm not sure I follow," he said. "A computer is going to tell me who my perfect mate is? Look, I'm all for new technology, but when it comes to a person's love life, that all sounds pretty cold to me."

She said, "Cold—hot—temperature doesn't come up on the app's questions."

"Then what does come up, Vivian? A criminal background check?" he asked, then burst out laughing at his own crude joke.

How to avoid jerks like you, Vivian wanted to say. Instead, she said through tight lips, "Those types of candidates will automatically be ejected from the system."

"That's good to know," Ted replied. "But I'm still looking for the flawless woman. Tell me exactly how My Perfect Match will find her?"

"I—think—" Her words trailed away in confusion and she darted a helpless glance at Wes.

Thankfully he picked up the rest of her sentence as though they'd planned it that way.

"I think what Vivian is trying to say is that My Perfect Match takes the doubt out of dating. It's all about being compatible, rather than a person's appearance or the chemistry between two people. Isn't that right, Viv?"

Smiling, he looked at her, and for a moment all Vivian could do was gaze into his eyes. She'd never noticed them being so blue before or so full of warmth.

"Oh—yes," she gushed. "Absolutely."

"Well, I must admit this is a new concept. And you definitely sound confident about its abilities," Ted said to Wes. "Would you be willing to trust your love life with My Perfect Match?"

"I certainly would," Wes said without a pause. "I'm more than happy to let the app tell me who I need to be dating."

The morning show host appeared completely amazed by Wes's announcement. "You mean you're telling me that *you* plan to use My Perfect Match?"

"I plan to start tomorrow."

Vivian's head jerked in Wes's direction. Had he lost his mind? To hear him tell it, everything he'd been spouting about the app was pure hogwash. Ted Reynolds and the viewing audience might not know it, but she certainly did. Why had Wes suddenly made such a wild promise? And on national TV!

"Did you hear that, folks? Wes Robinson isn't afraid to put himself on the dating market! He's just vowed to use My Perfect Match to find his perfect lady. I can promise you that *Hey, USA* will certainly be following the outcome of this romantic venture!"

While Vivian was trying to make sense of what had just happened, the interview wrapped up. And even after a crew member removed her earpiece, she continued to sit watching dazedly as the broadcast crew carried its equipment out of Wes's office.

Once the room was finally quiet again, Wes walked over to the wall of plate glass and let out a hefty sigh.

As Vivian watched him stare moodily out at the city, she forced herself to her feet. The past few minutes had twisted her nerves so tight she felt utterly drained, and for a moment she wondered if her legs would hold her upright.

"Well, that turned out to be a hell of a mess," he said.

Vivian winced with regret. Of course he was disgusted. She'd let him down in a big way and made herself look like an imbecile in the process.

"I'm sorry," she told him. "I've never done anything like this before. The second we went on the air, my mind went blank. And Ted Reynolds wasn't helping matters. He was—"

She was searching for the right word when Wes found it for her.

"Being an ass," he finished.

She took a few tentative steps forward until she was standing close enough to see his brows pull into a scowl.

"You noticed?" she asked.

"Hell yes, I noticed."

Realizing she was twisting the frames of her eyeglasses, she eased her grip and thrust her hands behind her. "Well, I'm not going to use him as an excuse for my breakdown. Everything I wanted to say about My Perfect Match came out wrong."

His expression a picture of frustration, he turned and closed the distance between them. "Forget about it, Vivian. It's over and done with. And frankly, what you said or how you said it doesn't matter now. I'm the one who came out of this looking like a fool."

Stunned that he was being so magnanimous about the whole thing, she stared at him. "You? What are you talking about? You didn't miss a beat. You made My Perfect Match sound like something every single person should purchase."

He rolled his eyes. "I realize you were visiting another planet during our interview, but surely you heard me say I'd be using the app for my own personal dating agenda."

She tried to keep the dismay she was feeling off her face. "I heard. But I don't understand your frustration. Ted Reynolds will never know if you use My Perfect Match. I doubt we'll hear from him or the show's producers again."

"If this was just a phony promise made to a jackass television host, I wouldn't care. But I was also speaking to a national audience. Many of whom purchase and use Robinson Tech products. They expect me to be forthright about myself and my company. Not to mention all the curiosity this is going to generate with the public. Everyone is going to be watching like a hawk to see what happens with me and this—dating thing of yours."

Vivian rubbed fingers against her furrowed brow. She should be happy that her boss had managed to get himself in such a predicament. His misery was fitting payback for all that ridicule of My Perfect Match he'd spouted to her yesterday. Yet surprisingly, seeing the harried tension on his face right now didn't give her the slightest feeling of satisfaction.

"I see what you mean," she said thoughtfully. "As a representative of Robinson Tech, you feel obligated to follow through on your promise."

"It's a relief to see your brain is working again, Ms. Blair."

One minute he used her first name and the next he reverted back to "Ms. Blair." His vacillation made her wonder how he thought of her. As Vivian the woman, or Ms. Blair the computer developer? Either way, she wanted to tell him she'd had enough of his insults for one day, but she'd already put her job in enough jeopardy with the interview debacle.

"Well, if that's the way you feel—I mean, if you're actually going through with your vow to use My Perfect Match, then it's only right that I use it, too. After all, I'm the one who has real confidence in the app."

With a faint smirk on his lips, he stepped closer.

"You? Use the app?"

The incredulous tone of his voice made her lift her chin to a challenging angle. "What's the matter? Afraid I'll prove you wrong about My Perfect Match?"

"I hope you do prove me wrong and this blasted thing turns out to be a roaring success," he countered, then slithered a skeptical look down the length of her body. "I just wasn't aware that you were looking for a perfect man."

I'm certainly not looking at him now. Vivian bit down on her tongue to keep the words from leaping out of her mouth.

"In this day and age, the task of finding a perfect man seems like a hopeless quest, but I've not given up the search," she said primly, then shoved her eyeglasses onto her face. "And now that I've created My Perfect Match, I feel much more hopeful of finding him."

The sly grin spreading over his lips was followed by a suggestive gleam in his blue eyes. One that left Vivian feeling so uncomfortable, she wanted to run out of his plush office as fast as her legs would carry her.

"Well, you've just made this whole fiasco more bearable and interesting. I'm willing to bet I find my perfect woman long before you find your perfect man."

Thrilled for the chance to prove him wrong, she stuck out her hand. "It's a deal."

His fingers curled firmly around hers, and Vivian tried to ignore the heat racing up her arm and stinging her cheeks with color.

"Great," he said. "May the best man win?"

The wry taunt in his voice put enough steel in her backbone to make a metal detector blow a fuse.

"You have it all wrong, Mr. Robinson. Let's hope *love* wins. For the both of us."

Wes stared thoughtfully after Vivian as she headed out the door. Adelle passed her on the way into his office.

Since the secretary didn't enter his private work space unless she had good reason, he knew something was up. Given the bad start to his day, he figured it wasn't good news.

While she walked briskly into the room, her high heels clicking with every step, Wes sank into the plush chair behind his desk and wiped a hand over his face.

"Okay, what's happened? It's nine forty-five in the morning and you look like you already need a stiff cocktail."

Stopping in front of his desk, she tapped the eraser of her pencil against the cherry wood. "You've really done it," she quipped. "How do you expect me to get any work done when my phone is jammed with calls?"

"Adelle, you knew this interview was happening this morning. I told you to inform everyone that I'd be late returning calls."

Her eyes rolled toward the ceiling. "Mr. Robinson,

these aren't your usual calls. This is coming from newspapers, television stations, radio and all sorts of media people. Everyone is buzzing with your announcement about My Perfect Match. I've been trying to put them off, but—"

"What do they want? If they're interested in doing advertising for the app, then you should direct their calls to advertising and marketing."

"Thank you for that helpful advice." She shot him a tired look, then asked, "How long do you think I've been working here? A week or two?"

"Probably as long as the world has had white thread," Wes said, not bothering to hide his impatience. He had more important things on his mind than listening to a lecture from his bossy secretary.

"That's right. Longer than you can count. I believe I've gotten the hang of how to direct calls," she informed him. "But I think you ought to know these calls are directed at your personal life. My impression is that the media plans to cover your so-called dates. You and the lucky lady will most likely be followed around like the hottest star of the week hounded by Hollywood paparazzi."

"Oh, damn!"

She thrust her pencil into the hair above her right ear. "*Oh, damn* is right. What were you thinking?"

Ever since the interview had wrapped, Wes had been asking himself that very question. He'd accused Vivian of momentarily losing her senses; well, he'd admittedly committed the same crime.

"Clearly, I wasn't," he muttered, then rubbed his fingers over his closed eyelids. "It's just that Ted Reynolds was doing his best to make a mockery of the app. I wanted to put him in his place."

And surprisingly, Wes had wanted to come to Vivian's defense. In spite of her ridiculous notions about finding everlasting love through a mobile app, he understood she'd worked long, tireless hours to get My Perfect Match to the public. She didn't deserve to have her effort ridiculed in front of a national television audience. And yet, there was a part of him that wanted to open her eyes and show her that love wasn't a cold, clinical pairing between a man and a woman. It was all about overwhelming attraction and desire. At least, that was how he wanted to imagine it. So far in his dating endeavors, he'd never experienced the euphoric state of mind called love.

"Hmm. I suppose if you find a woman who fits you like a glove, you'll make Ted Reynolds look like more of a fool than he already is. Add to that, you'd prove Vivian's theory about compatibility right. Which would be a good thing," Adelle mused aloud. "And now that Ben is about to get married, it's your turn to look for a wife."

Wes grunted. "It's not a written law that twins have to do everything alike, you know."

The cell phone on Wes's desk suddenly rang, preventing Adelle from flinging a disapproving remark at him. He picked up the phone to answer the call, but noticed she was already on her way out of the office.

"Just a minute, Adelle."

Pausing at the door, she glanced back at him. For some odd reason, Wes suddenly wondered how the secretary had looked when she was Vivian's age. Had she been madly in love with her husband? Or had the guy been like Wes's father, Gerald? Unworthy of a good woman's love? What if the dating app led Vivian to such a scoundrel?

"Was there something else?"

Adelle's question had Wes mentally shaking himself. Vivian's personal life was no concern of his. If any of her matches turned out to be cads, then that would be her problem.

"Yes, there was. Concerning my self-test of My Perfect Match, you can inform the media outlets I'll be starting tomorrow. Oh, and you might also relay the message that Vivian will also be using the app—to find her perfect man," he added drily.

Adelle looked at him with dismay. "Vivian? And you approve of that?"

Wes frowned. "Why would I disapprove?"

"Well, why indeed?" she asked with a smirk. "That sweet little thing thrown out there among all those wolves? I shudder to think who she might get tangled up with."

Wes found it hard to imagine Vivian getting tangled up in the bedsheets with any man. She was too prim and calculating to have such a reckless encounter. "Believe me, Adelle, sweet little Vivian, as you call her, knows exactly what she's doing."

With a roll of her eyes, the secretary left the room, and Wes turned his attention to the phone in his hand. Before he could scroll through the call log, the face lit up with another call.

Seeing it was Ben, he drew in a bracing breath and took a seat. No doubt his twin had already heard about Wes's declaration to use the dating app and was rolling on the floor with laughter. Well, Ben could do all the goading he wanted, Wes thought as he swiped to answer the call. When all was said and done, presenting his brother with a hefty sales number from My Perfect Match would shut him up.

* * *

When Vivian got back to Research and Development, George and Justine were waiting at her cubicle. From the guarded looks on their faces, she could tell they'd watched the live remote.

Holding up a hand to ward off their remarks, she said, "You don't have to tell me. I was a complete disaster."

George gave her a sympathetic pat on the shoulder. "It wasn't all that bad."

"Not at all," Justine chimed in. "And you looked great with your hair like that."

Vivian shot her a confused look, then quickly patted the top of her hair. "Like what? Is it all mussed up?"

"No," Justine said with a giggle. "The way it's tucked behind your ear. Gives you a really chic look."

Just the thought of Wes's infuriating remarks had Vivian quickly shaking her hair loose. "My hair was—just a mistake. And my mouth was even worse," she added with a groan of misery. "Every word that passed my lips made me sound like an idiot! I've probably ruined any hope that My Perfect Match will be a big seller."

"I wouldn't think that," George spoke up. "Uh, so what did Mr. Robinson say afterward?"

Before Vivian could answer George's question, Justine pelted her with another.

"Probably angry, huh?"

Exhaling a long breath, Vivian moved past her coworkers and practically flopped into her desk chair. "Not exactly. I mean, Wes—uh, Mr. Robinson—isn't the type to show much emotion. Have you two ever seen him angry?"

George and Justine both shook their heads.

Justine said, "We're not as lucky as you, Viv. We rarely meet with the man."

"I'm fine not to meet with him," George put in. "Makes me nervous to have to talk to the boss."

Justine made a dismissive gesture with her hand. "Technically, he's not our boss, George."

"Don't kid yourself," George said drily. "You mess up with Wes Robinson and you'll be outta here."

"His twin, Ben, is the new COO. And from what I hear, Wes was pretty hacked off that he didn't get the job."

Her nerves already frazzled, Vivian massaged the pain gathering in the middle of her forehead. "Justine, please, give it a rest. Anybody in this building with the name Robinson is our boss. Plain and simple. Now if you two will excuse me, I need to get to work."

"Oh? Orders from *our* boss?" Justine asked slyly.

Dropping her hand, Vivian looked at her coworkers. She might as well let them in on her plan, she decided. They were going to hear about it sooner or later anyway.

"Not exactly. I'm signing up on My Perfect Match. The quicker, the better."

"What?" George stared at her with real concern.

Justine giggled. "You? On My Perfect Match? Are you kidding, Viv?"

"Not in the least. Wes is willing to give it a try. So am I."

The concern on George's face grew deeper as he walked over to Vivian and looked down at her. "Are you doing this just because he is?"

Was she? When Vivian had first come up with the concept of My Perfect Match, she'd certainly not been creating the app for her own personal use. In spite of everything she'd said to Wes, she still wanted to meet her suitors the old-fashioned way. After that, she'd make the decision whether they were completely compatible or not. But when Wes had insisted he was actually going to use the app, she realized she had to step up to the plate and do the same.

"If a person isn't willing to use her own product, George, what kind of impression is that going to give the public? I've got to show Wes and everyone that I believe in this thing."

"Good thing you're not a casket maker," Justine quipped.

George shot the other woman a tired look, then shook his head at Vivian. "Are you sure you know what you're doing, Viv?"

To answer his question, Vivian picked up her smartphone and scrolled through the pages of applications until she found My Perfect Match.

"I've never been more certain. I'm going to find the man of my dreams. Our likes and dislikes will match precisely. We'll have no choice but to fall in love and live happily ever after."

Justine let out a mocking groan. "Oh, please. That's enough to send me back to work."

George must have had the same thought because he turned to follow Justine out of the small cubicle.

"What? No words of wisdom from you, George?"

Looking over his shoulder, the burly redhead frowned at her. "All I can say is good luck, Vivian. You're going to need it."

Scowling back at him, she asked, "What is that supposed to mean?"

"Just that you've set your goals mighty high."

"Somewhere out there is the man I want to spend the rest of my life with. And My Perfect Match is going to find him for me."

"Hmm. Well, if that's the case, then Wes Robinson is going to find the woman he wants to share the rest of his life with. So this app should make you both very happy."

Happy? Oh, yes, Vivian thought, proving Wes wrong was going to make her ecstatic.

Chapter Four

"Vivian, are you sure you know what you're doing?"

How many times had she heard that in the past two days? The question was becoming a broken record, Vivian thought.

Not bothering to look over at her sister, Michelle, who was standing a few steps away, watching as Vivian applied a coat of mascara to her already dark lashes. Normally she didn't use a great deal of makeup when going on a date, but tonight was special. Or at least she was treating it as such. Tonight was her first date generated by My Perfect Match and she wanted to make a good impression.

"I'm going on a dinner date," she answered, trying her best to sound casual even though her nerves were balled in a knot.

"With someone you've never met before." Michelle shook her head in dismay. "You're far braver than me, sis."

She wasn't brave, Vivian thought. Determined was more like it. "I have to start somewhere. And it's just dinner."

"As far as I'm concerned, you should've never made such a wager with Wes Robinson," she argued. "And just what are you going to get if you prove the app works? A bonus from Robinson Tech? Bragging rights?"

Vivian turned away from the dresser mirror to glance at her sister. Three years older, Michelle was a few inches taller and several pounds lighter than Vivian. Michelle had curly chestnut hair and pale, porcelain skin, and Vivian had always considered her sister to be far prettier than her. And as a high school art teacher, Michelle was far better at communicating with people.

Using the mascara wand to punctuate her words, Vivian said, "Neither of those things. I'm going to get a man. One I can build a family with. One I can depend on to be around for the long haul."

Michelle groaned. "Sis, you ought to consider making a job change. Computers can do a lot of things, but they can't keep a man faithful or responsible."

"Maybe not. But they can weed out the worst of the worst. Besides, I don't exactly see you making any wedding plans." Vivian turned back to the mirror and carefully dabbed on a small amount of lip gloss. Behind her, Michelle walked over to the bed, where Vivian had laid out a brown mid-calf skirt, a white shirt and a camel-beige cardigan to go over it. No doubt her sister was wondering why she'd not chosen something more colorful to wear.

"You're the one who wants a husband," Michelle reasoned. "I enjoy being single and independent—like Mom. When the right man comes along, I'll know it. I don't need a computer to tell me."

Vivian's freshly glossed lips pressed into a thin line. "Thanks for the vote of confidence in my work," she said with a heavy dose of sarcasm. "And open your eyes, sis. Mom doesn't like being single. She's simply too afraid to try marriage again."

"Bah! After the way Dad treated her, she has no interest in being married. If you ask me, she was relieved after she and Dad divorced."

Vivian sighed. "They had nothing in common."

"Only three kids," Michelle said wryly.

Vivian stepped into the skirt and zipped it up, then reached for the shirt. "And we obviously weren't enough to hold them together."

Michelle grimaced. "Well, no. Not when one spouse goes looking for love elsewhere."

Vivian stared at her as she dealt with the buttons on her shirt. "What are you saying?"

Michelle shrugged, then cast a sheepish look at her sister, as though she wished she'd not mentioned anything regarding their father.

"Dad was always on the road," she said. "He had a wandering eye and Mom knew it."

"You don't know that for sure."

"No," Michelle admitted. "But he married very quickly after the divorce was final."

"Some men are needy."

"Exactly my point."

Shaking her head, Vivian said, "I really don't need to hear this sort of thing tonight, Michelle. In fifteen minutes, I'm going to open the door to a man I've never met before, and I don't want to be eyeing him as though he's already under suspicion."

"Oh!" Michelle glanced at her wristwatch. "He's going to be here in fifteen minutes? I'd better go. I don't want to be a distraction. Besides, I have a stack of test papers to grade."

She hurried around to the other side of the bed and smacked a kiss on Vivian's cheek. "Good luck, sissy. Let me know how things go with the search for Mr. Right. And in case you don't know—I'm proud of you."

Twenty minutes later, Vivian stood at the open door of her apartment, her neck bent backward as she peered up at her first date. She'd seen shorter basketball players, she decided, but with his extremely thin frame, he'd be crushed the first time he attempted to make a goal. As for his face, she couldn't tell much about his eyes. They were hidden behind a pair of thick-lensed glasses. The rest of his features were lean to the point of being bony and as solemn as a man who'd just received a death sentence.

The app considered this man an attractive match for her?

Remember, Viv, this isn't about attraction. This is all about likes and dislikes.

"Good evening," she greeted him, hiding her dismay as best she could. "Are you Paul Sullivan?"

He gave her a slight nod. "Yes. Are you Vivian Blair?"

"I am."

"Good. I wasn't sure the GPS in my vehicle was working properly. And the signal on my cell phone loses its mind on this side of town."

And based on her first impression of this man, before this night was over, there was a real possibility that Vivian might lose hers.

Smiling, she said, "Well, you're here, and on time, too. If you'll step inside, I'll get my things and we'll head on to the restaurant."

* * *

By the time Vivian and Paul had finished their salads and started on the main course, Vivian had learned he was an IT technician for a large insurance company. He had four brothers and one sister, all of whom lived in Michigan. Two years ago, his current job had lured him to Austin, but so far the Texas heat had caused him to suffer several heat strokes. A fact that had him dreading the coming spring.

"Perhaps you'll get acclimatized soon," Vivian offered on a hopeful note.

"I doubt it. Everyone tells me you have to be tough to live in Texas."

And Paul Sullivan definitely didn't fit that category, she thought as she pushed her fork into a fillet of grilled tilapia.

"Well, the natives are born that way," she said, her mind drifting to Wes. Was he out on the city tonight, she wondered, squiring around his first date? What sort of woman would the app match him with? Some sort of computer genius? Or maybe a refined woman of the arts who was familiar with his social circles?

Paul's voice broke into her thoughts.

"Yes, that's why I'll probably be heading back home to Michigan soon. I'm afraid another summer here might kill me."

"Oh. That's too bad."

He peered candidly at her. "You mean you wouldn't be willing to move there—with me?"

Vivian nearly choked on a bite of fish. "Uh—no. Texas is my home."

He looked completely dumbfounded. "Oh. But I thought—you see, the app says the two of us are perfectly aligned. That means we'd be happy together no matter where we live."

Oh, Lord, if this was the best the app could offer, she was in big trouble.

"Paul, I think—"

She paused, deciding it would be useless to explain that being technically matched to someone didn't necessarily mean instant commitment. It would only burst his hopeful bubble. And wasn't that what My Perfect Match really stood for? she asked herself. The hope of finding someone to love?

"Yes?" he asked eagerly.

Smiling wanly, she said, "I was just going to say I think I won't have dessert tonight. But feel free to enjoy some if you'd like."

Across town, in a skyline restaurant located in one of the finest hotels in Austin, Wes stared across the table for two at the woman sipping a fruity cocktail. Earlier this evening as he'd showered and changed, he'd been thinking he'd rather be rolled over by a piece of highway equipment than meet Miss Perfect Match.

But later, when the hostess had shown his match to his table, he'd nearly fallen out of his chair. The expectations of his first date had vacillated wildly between a career woman with a scientific mind and a blonde bimbo with an ample show of cleavage. Mercifully, Julia's appearance was neither.

Pretty and friendly, she could even carry on a decent conversation. Perhaps Vivian was on to something with this compatible thing, Wes thought.

Vivian. Earlier today, she'd sent him an email message informing him she was going on her first date tonight. Wes had replied that he'd be doing the same.

Now, as he sipped his drink and the smooth whiskey slid warmly down his throat, he wondered where his developer was tonight and what sort of man the app had picked for her. A muscle-bound athlete with roaming hands, or a suave businessman with a line of phony charm? As far as he was concerned, either image was wrong for her. But then, he didn't think like a computer. Even though his family business was all about the mechanical brains.

"Wes, have I already lost you?"

His date's question brought him out of his thoughts, and he mentally shook himself as he gave her the most charming smile he could muster.

"Sorry, Julia, I was thinking about a project at work."

"Wondering if it will succeed?"

"Something like that."

Smiling provocatively over the rim of her cocktail glass, she said, "I'm certain whatever you're working on will be a winner. The app implies you're a brilliant man."

The app might consider him brilliant, but apparently his father didn't, Wes thought ruefully. At least, not brilliant enough to handle being COO of Robinson Tech. And Vivian—well, she believed his ideas about love were totally ignorant.

But why the hell should he care what Vivian thought about him? She was just a company developer. One of many. And as for his father, he might be one of a kind, but he was the kind Wes didn't want to emulate.

"I'm not sure my work will turn out to be a winner," he said smoothly. "But tonight I feel like one."

Julie laughed, and as Wes drained the last of his drink, a vision of Vivian's disapproving face entered his mind.

She wouldn't go for a line like that, Wes thought. No, that sweet little thing, as Adelle called her, was too smart and stiff to be swayed by a man's glib tongue.

Or was she? The man she was with tonight was supposed to be her kind of guy. He might know the exact words to say to soften her defenses and lure her into his bed.

Bed? No! Not Vivian! For some reason his mind refused to conjure up such a vision.

"Wes? Are you okay?"

He blinked and then, realizing she'd caught him daydreaming for a second time, he felt a wash of embarrassment creep up his neck.

"Sure," he said with feigned innocence. "Why?"

The young woman's gaze zeroed in on the squatty tumbler he was holding. "You're gripping your glass so hard, I'm afraid it's going to shatter in your hand."

Practically dropping the glass to the tabletop, Wes used his forearm to shove it aside, then forced himself to lean attentively toward her.

"Sorry," he apologized again. "I'm just not—myself this evening. But I promise to give you my undivided attention for the remainder of it. Now, tell me all about yourself."

The next morning, Vivian was staring at her computer screen, trying to focus on the work she should've finished yesterday, when a folded newspaper was suddenly thrust in front of her face. The hand holding it was wearing an onyx ring, and the shock that Wes Robinson had bothered to come to her work cubicle had her whirling the chair around to face him.

"What—is something wrong?" she practically sputtered.

A smug expression curved one corner of his mouth, and she instantly wondered if his first date had received a kiss from those same privileged lips.

"Not as far as I'm concerned."

He handed her a folded copy of the *Texan Gazette*. "Page twenty-four in the social section."

Vivian quickly fumbled through the pages. When she reached the right page and spotted a picture of herself and Paul, her mouth fell open.

"That's me!" she said with a shocked gasp. "We were leaving the restaurant. I had no idea anyone was watching us. This is creepy!"

"Creepy or not, it happened. And why the surprise? After our national exposure, you should have known the local media would pick up on our venture."

"I didn't say anything during that interview about personally using the app!" she protested. "You did!"

His expression turned sly. "The media has a way of finding out these things."

Her jaw dropped. "You told them!"

He chuckled, and it dawned on Vivian that he was enjoying this whole charade. The idea was even more surprising than finding a photo of herself in an Austin newspaper.

"Why should I be the only one hounded by the press?" He tapped a finger on another photo at the top of the page. "Apparently you didn't notice this one."

Her gaze followed the direction of his finger, and as she studied the image, she felt herself going hot and then cold.

"Wes Robinson, son of tech mogul Gerald Robinson, was spotted at the Capital Arms Restaurant last evening with a computer-inspired date."

After reading the caption beneath the photo, Vivian glanced up at Wes. "This was your date?"

"That's Julia," he said smugly. "I have to admit, Vivian, so far your app seems to understand exactly what I want in a woman."

Vivian turned her attention back to the photo. Wes's date could easily pose for the cover of a fashion magazine. And the alluring expression she was casting at Wes must have sent him into a dreamy stupor. Vivian had never seen her boss looking so dazed.

Vivian should have been jumping for joy that the app had worked for him, at least. Instead, she felt almost queasy. As if she'd taken a dose of painkillers on an empty stomach. "So you two communicated well?"

"Absolutely. She was smart, funny, interesting—I'm beginning to wonder if I should just stop right now and call her the winner."

The triumphant note in his voice irked her to no end. "Really? One date is all you need to decide she's your perfect mate?"

"I only said I was wondering, not quitting. Besides, if my next dates turn out to be as charming as Julia, why should I stop such a fun quest?"

He'd had fun and she'd gone home with a headache. There was nothing fair about this, Vivian thought miserably.

"Good for you," she retorted. "But frankly, this image of your date has me doubting your honesty."

His eyes narrowed, and Vivian noticed they were abnormally bloodshot this morning, as though he'd downed too much alcohol or had a very late night. Both a product of blonde Julia, she figured.

"What are you talking about? I'm not going to lie about my dates." He pointed to the newspaper image.

"You can see for yourself that she's an attractive woman. I could hardly make that up."

"I'm not doubting that you had a good time on your date last night. I'm just wondering if you answered the questions on My Perfect Match truthfully. What did you put down as your occupation? That you run a modeling agency?"

His short laugh was mocking. "What did you put down as your occupation? That you're a scout for the NBA?"

Disgusted now, she tossed the paper onto her desk. "Very funny. I should expect you to say something like that! You know, Mr. Robinson, not everyone is as flawless as you."

"So you didn't mind breaking a vertebra in your neck to look up at him?"

"For your information, I didn't break a thing," she said coolly.

"So do you plan on seeing him again?"

Not in a thousand years, Vivian silently answered. To Wes she said, "I don't know who I'm going to date next. I'm going to let the app decide that for me."

A clever grin curved the corners of his lips. "Yes, maybe we'd better let the app do its work. That is what this is all about."

"Exactly."

He turned to leave, then pointed to the newspaper. "By the way, you can keep that for a souvenir. I expect it will be one of many. Oh, and don't you think you should start calling me Wes? Now that we're in a dating battle, so to speak, it sounds ridiculous for you to call me Mr. Robinson."

She couldn't have been more shocked. In the past six years she'd worked for the guy, he'd never invited her to be personal with him. But then, they'd never worked on such a personal project together before.

"You are my superior," she reminded him.

"Don't let that stop you."

"All right, Wes."

He gave her a thumbs-up and left the cubicle.

Relieved, Vivian slumped back in her chair and reached for the newspaper. For two cents, she'd push the thing into the paper shredder. The last thing she wanted was a reminder of her disastrous date. And as for Wes's escapade last evening, she wasn't going to waste one more second wondering if he'd spent his night in the arms of the beautiful blonde.

On Friday evening, Wes was standing at the elevator a few doors down from his office when he heard Ben's voice call out to him.

"Hey, Wes! Wait up."

Glancing down the corridor, he spotted his twin stride quickly toward him. The elevator doors chose that exact moment to open, but Wes ignored them and waited for his brother to join him.

"Looking for me?" Wes asked.

"I tried your cell earlier and Adelle wasn't answering her phone. When you didn't pick up your office phone, I was beginning to think you were sick." He eyed the worn leather bomber jacket Wes was wearing this evening. "And you must be if you're quitting work this early in the evening."

Wes punched the down button and the doors opened again. This time Wes stepped inside with Ben following close behind him.

"Sorry about the cell phone. These past few days, I've had to silence the ringer. The constant sound was driving me nuts. But as to my health, I'm actually feeling great. Never better."

With no one else joining them in the elevator, Wes leaned forward to punch the number for the parking garage, and the car moved swiftly downward.

"Hmm. Well, you should be feeling on top of the world," Ben replied. "Marketing informs me the orders are pouring in for the new dating app. It appears all this publicity you've been doing is paying off. Good work, brother."

Wes eased back the cuff of his jacket to glance at his watch. He had less than fifteen minutes to meet his fourth app date at a nearby coffee shop. Normally, Wes didn't cut his schedule so close, but he'd spent the past hour going over cost data for a new processor his department had developed. Since his father had requested the information delivered to him before quitting time, Wes had worked all day going over the numbers, making sure Gerald Robinson could find no gaps in the report. No. Wes wasn't about to let the man find him making a mistake. Not in his work. Or his personal life.

"I wouldn't call it work," Wes told his twin. "It's dating."

Ben let out a low chuckle. "I honestly didn't know you had it in you."

Wes darted him a sharp look. "Had what in me?"

"The ability to land all those good-looking women. How many have you gone out with so far? Three? Four? And from the pics I've seen in the papers, they've all looked pretty darn attractive."

"Hey, you'd better not let Ella hear you saying that," Wes jokingly warned. "She might want to think twice about going through with next Saturday's wedding."

Ben chuckled again. "Ella knows I only have eyes for

her. And speaking of the wedding, that's why I stopped by your office. I wanted to remind you about rehearsal. At the church tomorrow night at seven. So you might want to cross off your dating schedule for tomorrow evening. It might be a little awkward to bring a computer date to a wedding rehearsal."

Leave it to his brother to suggest Wes would do something that crass. True, he wasn't the cool 007 that Ben was, but he knew where and when to show up with a lady on his arm.

Deliberately ignoring Ben's suggestion, Wes asked, "I assume we're having dinner afterward?"

"At the River Plaza."

One of the ritziest hotels in town, Wes thought. When Ben had said he wanted to give Ella everything, he'd obviously meant it.

"Will Dad be there?"

After a long pause, Wes glanced over at Ben. As their gazes locked, Wes knew they were both thinking of their childhood days and how their father had rarely been around for any family event. Instead of looking to their wandering father for male guidance and affection, the twins had always relied on each other. And in many ways that hadn't changed.

Ben exhaled a long breath and wiped a hand over his face. "No. He's leaving tomorrow afternoon for a convention in Chicago. A three-day affair."

Emphasis on *affair*, Wes wanted to say. Typical Gerald Robinson, business and personal pleasure before family. But he kept the snide remark to himself. This was an important time in Ben's life. His brother didn't need to be reminded of their father's shortcomings.

"Sorry, Ben."

He shrugged. "Yeah, well, the old man has promised to be at the wedding. And considering how he feels about this Fortune family search I've undertaken, I'm surprised he's agreed to attend. He's not a bit happy with me, you know."

"Well, not everyone in the Robinson family is happy with this endeavor of yours. But that doesn't mean we've stopped loving you."

The elevator came to a halt, and they stepped onto the dimly lit concrete floor of the parking garage. Wes gestured in the direction of his car. "My car is over there. Was there anything else on your mind? I'm supposed to meet the lady in fifteen minutes and need to get going."

"So you really are headed out on a date," Ben stated the obvious.

"That's right. She's driving up from San Antonio."

"There aren't enough women in Austin for you?"

Wes smirked. "The app is doing the choosing. Not me."

"Ah yes, the app," Ben said with a chuckle. "Well, good luck, brother. Maybe tonight's date will be *the* one."

Wes wasn't looking for *the* one. He'd watched their father make a mockery of marriage far too long to want to jump into matrimony himself.

"I'm sure you'll read about it in tomorrow's paper." Lifting a hand in a gesture of parting, Wes strode off in the direction of his car.

On the following Monday afternoon, Vivian sat staring at the small square logo displayed on her smartphone screen and wondered if she'd created a monster instead of a dreamland of everlasting love. The notion behind the red-and-silver key that represented My Perfect Match was to unlock the secrets of undying love. And once the logo was tapped by an eager finger, it unfurled to show a romantic image of two golden wedding bands bound together on a bed of white velvet.

Everything about the design and the meaning behind it had seemed textbook. That is, until Vivian had started using it. Now she felt as if she'd stepped into a nightmare. One she couldn't escape. Had she been wrong all along about finding a compatible mate? Was Wes right about two people needing a fire between them to make a relationship work? If so, then he was going to win their little wager. Even worse, My Perfect Match would be a total failure.

"We have five minutes left of our break. Are you going to spend it staring at your phone?"

The question came from Justine, who was sitting across the utility table, sipping on a canned soda. Today Vivian's coworker was wearing a tight black sweater and a red skirt that molded to her hips. If the neckline on her sweater had been a half inch lower, the office manager probably would've sent her home for not following proper dress code. But Justine was one to push the envelope and every once in a while, like this very moment, Vivian wished she could be a bit more like risky Justine.

"I'm not staring at my phone," Vivian corrected her. "I'm thinking."

Justine chuckled. "Trying to decide which one of those losers you want to go out with again?"

Vivian glared at her. "That's an awful thing to say. All of my dates have been polite gentlemen."

"A nice way of calling them dull."

Unfortunately, Justine couldn't have been more right. These past few nights, Vivian had been bored out of her mind and wondering how she could endure another evening trying to meet her Mr. Perfect.

After sipping her coffee and realizing it was on the verge of getting cold, she rose to her feet to toss it into the nearest wastebasket.

"Well, I'm not giving up," she told Justine. "Sooner or later, an interesting and good-looking guy will show up. After all, these men are being pulled from the test pool. Once the app goes on sale on Valentine's Day, then the playing field will widen considerably."

"You hope. From what I've seen in the papers, Wes doesn't need a deeper pool of dating candidates to choose from. He looks like he's doing mighty fine."

"He's been lucky," Vivian retorted.

Her phone suddenly chirped, notifying her that she had an incoming text message. Vivian tossed the foam coffee cup, then retrieved the phone from the tabletop.

Come to my office. Now.

What did he want? To gloat, Vivian thought.

Across the table, Justine studied her closely. "What's wrong? You look like you could bite the head off a nail."

If Vivian had an angry look on her face, it was because she was disgusted with the way her heart had suddenly skipped a beat at the thought of seeing Wes again. What was wrong with her, anyway? She'd worked with the man for six years, and in his presence the only thing she'd ever had on her mind was whether he'd approve of her work. But now, that damn app and all their talk about romance and dating and marriage had made her take a second look at him. And instead of seeing her boss, she was seeing a man. A most dangerous thing to be doing. Especially if she expected to hold on to her job and her senses.

"I have to go to Wes's office. Would you stop by

George's desk and tell him as soon as I finish I'll help him work on the equation he needs?"

"Sure, Viv."

Slipping her phone in the pocket of her sweater, she hurried out of the break room.

Although Wes had never been as much of a playboy as Ben, he'd always felt comfortable around women. He couldn't remember a time when he'd felt tongue-tied or nervous about meeting one. Which was a good thing, considering that this past week, he'd been meeting women who were total strangers. But this idea he was going to present to Vivian had turned his mouth to West Texas sand.

What if she refused? He'd look like a total idiot.

The light rap on the door had him looking away from the window to see Vivian entering his office. A dark gray skirt fluttered against her knees, while a white silk blouse was tucked inside the tiny waistband. The clothes could hardly be described as sexy, but as he watched her stride toward him, he decided there was something very charming about the way she looked in them.

"Hello, Vivian." He motioned for her to join him at the wall of glass. "Come look."

When she reached his side, he pointed to a bare-limbed hackberry tree in the small patch of ground behind the building. "A pair of mourning doves is back at the nest. They're getting ready to raise another brood."

"I didn't realize you were a bird watcher," she said.

"I'm not. About a year ago, while I was standing here at the window, I just happened to notice these two. They have a nest in a fork of that big limb on the right side of the tree trunk."

She leaned closer to the window. While she searched

for a glimpse of the nest, Wes found himself looking at the way her warm brown hair was pulled carelessly back from her face and how her lips had a hint of raspberry color on them.

"You couldn't know it's the same doves," she reasoned.

"I might keep my head stuck in a computer most of the time, but I do know a little about the outdoors. Doves usually go back to the nest they've used before. And they're like coyotes or wolves. Once they mate, they're together for life."

"Too bad the human species doesn't possess the same devotion."

The bitter tone in her voice surprised Wes. Had she been hurt in the past by an unfaithful lover? Or was she simply talking about society in general? Either way, now wasn't a good time to pursue those types of questions.

"Well, I think devotion got pushed aside by our higher intelligence," he murmured thoughtfully.

She smelled like a flower after a soft rain. Without consciously knowing it, he'd come to associate the unique scent with her. But then, these past few days, he'd begun to notice all sorts of little things about Vivian that he'd never taken the time to notice before.

He was studying the curtain of hair resting against her back when she suddenly turned from the window and speared him with a questioning look.

"I don't think you called me to your office to discuss the mating habits of mourning doves, did you?"

He cleared his throat. "No. I wanted to talk with you about something else."

Concern marked her brow. "Has something gone

wrong with the app?" she asked quickly. "A glitch in distribution? What—"

He held up a hand before she could go any further. "As far as I know, everything is still a go for the Valentine's Day roll out. Don't worry. Our techs will make sure every available buyer can easily download the app."

She let out a breath of relief, and he wondered if her worry over My Perfect Match was mostly for her own investment in the project, or his.

"Okay. I won't worry," she said. "So you must want to talk about my dates—or yours?"

"No." Even though his dates had been pleasant these past few nights, he wasn't the sort who wanted to be out and about every night of the week. Yet with the media lurking around every corner, he knew if he suddenly stopped appearing around town with a woman on his arm, everyone would suspect he'd found *the* one. The whole thing was getting monotonous. "This is about something else."

"Oh. You have a new project in mind for me or the team to work on?"

"No. Let's sit."

He gestured toward a long, wine-colored couch positioned a few feet away. He followed her over to the couch, then took a seat a few inches down from her. The wary expression on her face made his nerves twist even tighter.

"Wes, if this isn't about the app or work, then what—"

"This is something more personal," he interrupted.

She scooted closer. As Wes took in the look of surprise on her parted lips, he had the crazy inclination to kiss her. What in hell was happening to him?

"Personal?"

He reached for her hand and held it between the two of his. "That's right. I want you to be my date. On Valentine's Day—my wedding date."

Chapter Five

"Date? Wedding?" Her heart pounding, Vivian stared at him in disbelief. "What are you talking about?"

"My brother Ben's wedding is taking place this coming Saturday. On Valentine's Day."

Her heart slowed enough to allow her to catch a decent breath. "Yes, I remember reading the announcement," she said. "I'll go out on a huge limb and guess you'll be in the wedding party."

A wan smile touched his face, and Vivian wondered exactly how he was feeling about his twin getting married. She'd heard the brothers were especially close. Although she'd never understood why. Yes, people talked of twins bonded with a connection that bordered on mystical. But she couldn't imagine such a link between Ben and Wes. Other than looking identical, they were very different. Everyone who worked under the roof of Robinson Tech knew that brash Ben didn't mind plowing over whatever stood in the way of what he wanted, while Wes was the quiet workaholic, content to let his achievements speak for him.

"I'll be standing as Ben's best man."

"Congratulations to your brother. And you," she added.

"Thanks. We had rehearsal over the weekend and let me warn you, it's going to be a massive wedding and reception."

"Warn me?"

"Well, yes. As my date, you—"

She quickly held up her free hand to interrupt him. "Your date? Just a minute, Mr. Ro—I mean, Wes. I don't understand any of this. Why are you asking me of all people to attend the wedding with you? Weddings are family affairs. You should be taking someone special as your date."

Releasing his hold on her hand, he turned his attention toward the windows and the darkening skyline, but she somehow doubted he had the approaching rain on his mind.

"Vivian, don't try to pretend ignorance. You have a good idea of how many hours I spend here in my office. Do you think I have time for a special woman in my life?"

"You don't stay here around the clock," she reasoned. "Besides, how would I know something that personal about you?"

He swiped a hand through his already rumpled hair, and Vivian was beginning to see that he wasn't enjoying any of this. In fact, she got the feeling that he'd thought of her as a last resort date. The notion stung.

"The rumor mill in this place works harder than a

cotton gin in September. If I had a steady, you'd know about it, that's for sure."

Vivian felt herself blushing. The idea that he believed she'd gossiped about his love life was worse than embarrassing. Whatever he might think, she didn't sit around mooning or chatting about him or his wealthy family.

"Maybe not. But you've had a string of steady dates these past few days. Surely the app can provide you with an appropriate date. Why turn to me?"

Turning his gaze back to her, he frowned. "Because it just wouldn't be right to take a strange woman from My Perfect Match to the wedding. She might get the wrong idea about the whole thing. Like I'm getting serious or something. You understand?"

Vivian figured she was gaping at him like some sort of idiot, but she couldn't help it. The more he talked, the worse it sounded.

"I'm afraid I do. You don't want any of your dates getting the impression that you might actually care about them—in a serious way," she added drily.

"That's right. And you being a woman—well, you know how weddings put romantic notions in your head."

"Not mine," she said stiffly.

He shot her a smile of relief. "Thank God you're different and above all that sentimental foolishness. I knew I could count on you to understand the situation."

Oh, yes, she was above it all, she thought sadly. Most men saw her as a practical woman. Not one to bend over his arm and kiss senseless.

Her gaze drifted to his lips. Well, she didn't want Wes Robinson's kiss anyway. To allow herself to dream such dreams about her boss would be like staring in a jewelry store window, pining for a ten-karat diamond. It just wasn't going to happen.

"So you don't think your family will get the idea that there's anything between us?"

He shook his head. "They'd never suspect anything serious going on between us. They know you work for the company."

Trying not to let a hint of sarcasm enter her voice, she said, "And you'd never have serious intentions toward an employee."

A frown pulled his brows together. "I have no intentions of getting serious about any woman. Much less an employee. That would spell nothing but trouble."

Trouble indeed, Vivian thought. She would have liked to grind her heel into the arch of his foot and tell him to go limp off into the sunset. But he was Wes Robinson, her boss. The guy who worked tirelessly. The guy who'd always supported her work and encouraged her imagination to fly into the technical future. If not for him, My Perfect Match would have been tossed into the trash heap with the rest of the department's failed designs and ideas. At the very least, she owed him a favor.

"Okay," she finally agreed. "I'll be your date for the wedding."

"Great. I'll give you all the particulars of when and where later. In the meantime, I should inform you that the women guests are encouraged to wear red. In honor of Valentine's Day. So you might keep that in mind while you're picking out something."

A blank look of despair must have come over her face, because he suddenly seemed to realize she'd never have anything in her closet worthy to wear to a Robinson family wedding.

"Uh, and don't worry about the cost of buying a gown. Just go to Anton's and charge whatever you need to my account."

By now Vivian was so dazed she couldn't decide whether to be insulted or thrilled. Anton's was a high-end department store in Austin. She couldn't afford to breathe the air inside the place.

Pride had her lifting her chin. "Thank you, but I'll find a dress on my own and pay for it myself."

"Nonsense. I'm the one who's put you in this spot. You shouldn't be out the expense of a dress. If it will make you feel any better, just think of it as a work assignment."

And why not? she thought sickly. He certainly was.

"I don't like this," she said frankly. "I don't like the idea of being something I'm not. Of being a decoy."

Vivian was shocked to see a grin spread across his face. Wes wasn't a man who grinned about anything. He smiled on occasion, but never grinned. The playful expression made him all the more appealing.

"I'm sure you can fake it for a few hours," he said.

Fake it? With him? How could she pretend to be his date when being near him made her feel as if she was on a very real one? Oh, this was all so crazy.

Desperate to put an end to the tangled trail of her thoughts, she rose to her feet. "Is that all? I should get back to work—George needs my help."

Rising, he walked her to the door. "No need to keep you any longer. Thank you, Viv. I really appreciate you helping me out."

"I'll do my best not to let you down." With a hollow feeling in the middle of her chest, Vivian left his office and hurried past Adelle's desk before the woman could stop her with small talk.

I have no intentions of getting serious about any woman.

For the remainder of the day, his words haunted her.

She couldn't understand why he'd made a point of telling her such a personal thing. She'd certainly never flirted with the man or made any kind of overture toward him. If he was afraid she might be setting her sights on him, then he was crazy. Nothing about him matched the attributes she wanted in a man. But clearly he'd felt the need to remind her that he was off limits to her or any woman.

The idea was humiliating. By the time her work day ended, she was determined to show him she had no desire to snag him or any business shark. She preferred to swim with her own kind.

On Saturday, shortly after noon, Wes drove slowly through the row of apartment buildings as he searched for Vivian's number. Before today, he'd had no idea where she lived. He'd expected to find her somewhere in the suburbs, in one of the newer apartment complexes that had sprung up in recent years. Now, he was a bit surprised to see she resided in a quaint older area of the city. The huge live oaks shading the yards and the rampant growth of ivy clinging to the brick walls told Wes the buildings had probably been here for longer than Vivian had been alive. But the streets were neat and clean. The sight of kids playing outdoors and the sound of dogs barking from front porches gave the neighborhood a homey feel. Far more than his private estate, which was surrounded by security fencing and locked behind wrought iron gates.

When he finally spotted a driveway marked with the number twenty-two, Wes pulled in and parked his car behind a little blue economy car. As he walked to the tiny porch, he noticed two young boys in the next yard.

They were tossing a football and laughing as though they didn't have a care in the world.

The sight of them had him thinking back to the days when he and Ben had been that age. They'd grown up as privileged children, never wanting for anything. Except the attention of their father.

Attention. Like hell, Wes thought with disgust. Gerald had been too busy hiding his true identity to give his eight legitimate children the devotion they'd needed and deserved. Now Ben seemed to believe it was important to prove Gerald was a long-lost member of the famous Fortune family. But as far as Wes was concerned, none of that mattered. Whether Gerald's name was Robinson or Fortune, he'd been a negligent father and a louse of a husband.

Shaking away the dismal thoughts, Wes punched the doorbell, then glanced over his shoulder to see the boys had stopped their game of toss and were standing side by side, staring at him. Apparently they'd never seen a man in the neighborhood wearing a tuxedo.

The opening door creaked. Wes turned back around to see Vivian standing on the threshold.

"Oh, it's you. I wasn't expecting you for another fifteen minutes."

When she failed to invite him in, he made an open gesture with his hands. "Shall I leave and come back in fifteen minutes?"

With a flustered groan, she pushed the door wide and invited him inside. "I'm sorry, Wes. Please come in. I'm almost ready."

He followed her through a tiny foyer, then made a sharp right turn into a small living room. As she came to a halt in the middle of the floor, Wes was only vaguely aware of his surroundings. His gaze was riveted on Vivian. Something had happened to her. She'd transformed from a professional little developer into a dazzling vision of beauty. One who was practically taking his breath away.

"Viv! You look—" *Gorgeous* was the word he wanted to use, but he didn't want to start the day off by making her feel uncomfortable. "Great," he finished, his gaze sweeping from her upswept hair all the down to the toes of her black high heels.

She turned in a full circle, and as the hem of her dress swayed provocatively against her trim ankles, he had to admit the back of her looked just as luscious as the front. The deep red dress clung to her perfect little curves as though it had been tailor-made to fit. The neckline formed a V low against her back, while the front stopped at a point just above the space between her breasts.

"It took me ages to choose it," she admitted. "And even after I got it home, I had my doubts. What do you think?"

Except for Ben's, Wes figured every male eye in the church was going to be on her. Dear Lord, he'd not been expecting anything like this. How was he going to keep his eyes off all that creamy, smooth skin? How was he going to keep remembering that Vivian was a pretend date and not a real one?

"The dress is nice. Very nice."

"I purchased shoes and a handbag, too. But don't worry. I paid for them myself." She gestured toward a floral couch pushed along the outside wall of the room. "Have a seat while I finish getting ready. It shouldn't take me long."

She hurried out of the room. After he'd taken a seat, he looked around at the simple furnishings and wondered if Vivian entertained much company. She didn't seem like the socializing sort, but outside work, he hardly knew her. If he had, he would have expected to see her change from a plain little daisy into this fully bloomed rose.

Maybe she'd brought one of her app dates here, Wes thought. Maybe they'd sat close together on the very couch he was sitting on. And maybe the man had tasted her lips. Had her cherry-colored mouth been cold and stiff or warm and inviting?

Wes was trying not to think about the answer to that question when Vivian reappeared and announced she was ready. He took the cream-colored cape she was carrying and slipped it around her bare shoulders.

"It's sunny outside, but the wind is cold," he warned as he fastened the garment with a row of rhinestone buttons.

For the next few minutes, as Wes's luxury car carried them toward the church located on the opposite side of town, Vivian stared thoughtfully out the passenger window. When Justine had learned she was going to Ben Robinson's wedding as Wes's date, Vivian had thought the woman was going to fall over in a dead faint. And her sister Michelle's reaction to the news had been loud squeals of excitement followed by words of warning.

"I hope you don't make the mistake of reading any importance into this, Viv. You'd only be asking for heartache to think a man like Wes could see you as a serious date."

Vivian had actually laughed at her sister's ridiculous concern. How could Michelle even think Vivian could foolishly fall for her rich boss? There was no way that could ever happen.

"You're awfully quiet, Viv. Are you dreading this?"

She glanced over at him, then immediately wished she hadn't. She'd never seen him dress in formal clothes before or go without his glasses for more than five minutes at a time. He looked incredibly handsome today with his dark, unruly waves brushed to one side and his jaws shaved clean of black stubble. The tailor-made tuxedo fit his long, lean torso perfectly, and the dark color made his appearance even more dashing.

"A little," she admitted. "I'm not sure how I'm supposed to act."

With his attention focused on navigating the car though busy traffic, he asked, "How do you mean?"

Flustered at his clueless attitude, she let out a long breath. "Wes, it's obvious I can't be myself. I'm not here with you today as your employee, am I?"

A scowl creased his brow. "Look, Viv, if anyone is crass enough to inquire about our situation, then tell them you're my date for the day. Nothing more, nothing less."

Oh, brother, that was going to be easier said than done, Vivian thought. She could only hope she wouldn't have to do much more than say a polite hello to his family members. Like she'd told him, she didn't relish the idea of being a decoy.

"All right," she said drolly. "I'll give you admiring glances, not dreamy ones. And I'll do my best to call you Wes rather than Mr. Robinson. Is there anything else I should know?"

"Not that I can think of. By the time we get to the church, it will be time for me to join the rest of the wedding party. The ushers should seat you somewhere just behind my family. Then, once the ceremony is over, I'll meet you out front and we'll head to the hotel for the reception. That's all there is to it."

Maybe for him, Vivian thought. But she felt as though she was about to step onto a huge stage in front of an audience of VIPs. And to make matters worse, she would have to ad-lib her part of the script.

Vivian flinched in surprise as Wes suddenly reached across the leather seat and wrapped his hand around hers.

"Don't worry. This will all be over soon."

Soon? Their afternoon together was only just beginning, and already Vivian could feel herself tumbling headlong into a situation she couldn't control.

By the time Wes and Vivian entered the church, the members of the wedding party were already gathering to make their way to a vestibule out of sight of the hundreds of guests who were already being seated in the main sanctuary. Wes used the brief moments to quickly introduce Vivian to Ben, younger brother Graham, and two of their sisters, Rachel and Zoe.

Once Vivian left the group to take her seat among the wedding guests, Wes's dark-haired little sister, Zoe, jerked him aside.

"Where did you find her?" she asked, her eyes sparkling with curiosity. "Is she one of your app dates?"

The question irked Wes. He didn't like the idea of anyone linking Vivian to the group of women he'd recently been parading around the city. "No. If you must know, nosy sis, Viv and I work together. She created My Perfect Match."

"Ah, that's why I thought I recognized her," Zoe said. "Photos of her have recently been in the papers. She certainly looks different in person. She's very lovely. Why haven't we seen you with her before now?"

Thankfully, Wes didn't have time to answer that question as the change in music gave the cue that the ceremony was about to begin. Everyone quickly fell into line, then promptly filed into the main sanctuary.

As Wes took his place next to his brother, he noticed the huge church was overflowing with family and guests. Up and down the massive hall and on either side of the altar, candles flickered, while red and white flowers seemed to be everywhere.

The music changed yet again, and to one side of the podium, a prominent singer with the Austin Philharmonic began to sing a song about everlasting love. As Wes tried to concentrate on the lyrics, his thoughts turned to Ben and Ella. His twin had always been focused on Robinson Tech and his career. He'd never expected Ben to make room in his life for a wife. But here he was, about to say his vows in front of hundreds of guests. Wes could only hope the words *love, honor* and *cherish* would hold more meaning for Ben than they had their father.

The song ended, and as another began, Wes's thoughts drifted to his parents, who were sitting on the first pew, directly behind Wes and Ben and a row of groomsmen. It often amazed him that his mother and father had been married for nearly thirty-five years. The two appeared as a couple at family and social functions but never spent special private time together. In fact, Wes had never seen any sort of affection displayed between his parents. Bearing eight of Gerald's children was proof that Charlotte had once loved her husband, at least physically. Whether she still held any sort of feelings for the man was difficult for Wes to determine. Sometimes he believed his mother suffered through his father's roaming ways simply because it was easier than getting a divorce and fighting over millions of dollars.

Oh, Lord, Wes wanted no such cold arrangement for himself. If he ever lost his mind long enough to take a wife, he'd want their marriage to be nothing less than warm and loving.

The music finally turned into the wedding march, and every head in the church turned to see the bride make her way down the flower-strewn aisle. Because Ella had no father, her mother, Elaine, walked at her daughter's side. Joining Ella on the opposite side was her little brother, Rory, who walked with the aid of braces and crutches. Yet his struggle with cerebral palsy was completely forgotten as everyone in the audience was focused on the pride and joy glowing on his face.

Moved by the sight, Wes watched Ben's profile. His brother's expression was an overflow of love and humility. In that moment, Wes realized for the first time how deeply Ben felt for Ella and her family.

The bride took her place next to the groom, and the minister immediately requested for all to bow their heads. After the long prayer, the singer stepped up for another song about love. By the time the couple finally got around to exchanging their vows, Wes's mind began to drift to Vivian. Somewhere behind him, she was sitting in that beautiful red dress, watching the ceremony. What was she thinking? That My Perfect Match was going to find the right man to put a ring on her finger?

The questions were rolling through Wes's mind at the same time Ben was pushing the ring onto Ella's finger. And suddenly, a different picture swam before his vision. Instead of seeing his brother or new sister-in-law, Wes was picturing himself pushing a wedding band onto Vivian's finger.

Stunned by the image, Wes snapped himself out of his daze just in time to hear the minister's next words.

"You may kiss the bride."

Something about seeing his twin become a married man must have done something to Wes, Vivian thought. Ever since the two of them had left the church and arrived at the reception, he'd been quiet and pensive, as though he was somewhere far away instead of in an elaborate ballroom at the Travis Grand Hotel.

"Hello again, Vivian. Would you care for a bit of company? It seems our twins have chosen to desert us, doesn't it?"

Vivian turned to see the female voice behind her belonged to the new bride, Ella Thomas Robinson. During the elaborate wedding ceremony, Vivian had looked on in awe while thinking the beautiful princess was becoming the wife of her handsome prince. Now that she was up close, Vivian still found it hard to keep from gawking at the woman's gorgeous wedding gown. Done in an intricate rose lace pattern, the dress had a close-fitting bodice with the back making a wide V all the way to her waist. Rows of tiny seed pearls edged the low neckline and the wrists of the long, tight sleeves, while the skirt hugged her hips before falling into a pool of rich fabric at her feet. A band fashioned of pearls and tiny white roses held a single tiered veil to her upswept auburn hair.

Even if Vivian had a whole entourage of beauty consultants, she could never look so lovely, she thought. Or was the beautiful aura surrounding Ella actually a product of love? If so, would she ever experience such a glow? Vivian wondered.

"It appears that way," Vivian agreed. "Wes went after more champagne and got distracted by his mother."

Ella's dreamy smile landed on her husband, who was standing several feet away with his father and several other men Vivian recognized as groomsmen.

"And Gerald has cornered Ben with business, no doubt. I suppose my father-in-law has forgotten what it's like to be just married."

Vivian had met Ella earlier, before she and Ben had cut the giant tiered wedding cake and taken their first dance around the room. She'd been surprised that the COO of Robinson Tech had chosen to marry a woman as young and down-to-earth as Ella. But on the other hand, it was easy to see how he'd fallen in love with the warm-hearted beauty.

"The wedding was the most beautiful ceremony I've ever seen," Vivian told her, then admitted with a rueful smile, "honestly, I was nervous about attending. I'm not used to rubbing shoulders with such important people."

Ella laughed lightly. "Believe me, when I first started dating Ben, I felt the same way. You'll soon find out that they're just people, too. Have you known Wes very long?"

So Ella had the idea that she and Wes were truly a couple, she thought miserably. What would the new bride think if she knew her brother-in-law had brought Vivian to the wedding only because she was a safe date who expected nothing from him?

Vivian tilted a fluted glass to her lips and hoped the bubbly champagne would help ease her knotted nerves.

"About six years," she answered, while instinctively turning her gaze back to Wes and his mother.

"That long!" Ella exclaimed. "Oh, my, he must be a slow worker. I—"

"Hey, can I join in on the fun?"

The British accent caught Vivian's attention, and she looked around to see a tall woman somewhere in her twenties walking up to Ella's side. Slender and elegant, she had straight brown hair, hazel eyes and a faint smile that held a hint of mystery. Vivian was instantly intrigued.

Ella quickly introduced the two women. "Vivian, this is Lucie Fortune Chesterfield. And Lucie, this is Vivian Blair, my brother-in-law's lovely date."

Vivian shook hands with the woman. "Nice to meet you, Lucie. Did you fly in for the wedding? Or do you live in Texas?"

"Lucie is originally from London," Ella inserted, then laughed and gestured for Lucie to explain further.

"But I've been staying in Horseback Hollow with relatives," Lucie went on. "My sister married a cowboy there, and they have a baby daughter. I can hardly resist spending time with my little niece."

"Lucie is the one who helped Ben locate his half brother, Keaton Robinson—or I should say, Keaton Fortune Robinson," Ella added slyly.

Totally confused by this information, Vivian looked from one woman to the other. "I don't understand. Half brother? I didn't realize there was a half brother."

Ella and Lucie exchanged a pointed look.

"Well, the connection was only discovered a few weeks ago," Ella told her. Then, with a curious expression, she asked, "Doesn't Wes talk with you about family matters?"

Vivian felt her cheeks grow warm with embarrassment. "Wes and I have been dealing with lots of work. I guess it slipped his mind."

"Well, then, you don't know that Ben is trying to prove their father, Gerald, is actually a member of the Fortune family?"

Clueless and not bothering to hide the fact, Vivian shook her head. "Fortune? Are you talking about the Fortunes who own the cosmetic company?"

"That's right," Ella answered.

Still perplexed, Vivian glanced at Lucie. "Then if your name is Fortune, you could be related to Wes and Ben."

"We're thinking that could be so."

Stunned by this news, Vivian glanced through the crowd until her gaze landed on Wes. Did she really know the man at all?

Across the room, Wes stood with his mother, Charlotte, as she sipped champagne and commented about the wedding ceremony. Ben was the first one of her children to finally get married, and though Wes had expected her to be happy about the event, she seemed rather pensive.

"What's wrong, Mother? The ceremony went off without a hitch. I don't know much about these sorts of things, but I thought everything looked pretty grand. And everyone appears to be having a good time at the reception. Aren't you happy for Ben and Ella?"

She touched a hand to her short platinum hair and Wes decided, for a woman in her midseventies, his mother looked at least ten years younger. Unlike the majority of female guests who'd worn red in some fashion today, Charlotte had opted to wear a pastel pink dress with a heavy dose of diamonds at her throat. He supposed she'd foregone wearing red in order to stand out in the crowd. Or, knowing his mother, she probably worried the color clashed with her complexion. Either way, nothing was missing about his mother's appearance, he concluded, except a happy smile.

Charlotte said, "This affair today is hardly what concerns me, Wes. Anyone with money and good taste can throw a decent party. No, it's Ben whom I'm thinking of now. I wish a thousand times he'd not jumped into this marriage so quickly. It's hardly been a month since he and Ella first got engaged!"

Wes held back a sigh. "Ben never was one to waste time, Mother. But I wouldn't worry about him. He's fully aware of what he's doing."

She glanced sharply up at him. "Are you?"

Taken slightly aback by her abrupt question, Wes frowned, then finally chuckled. "I like to think so. Why do you ask?"

Her lips pursed with disapproval, and Wes could only wonder what was going on in her mind. He loved his mother dearly. She'd always been the glue that held the Robinson family together. She'd always been the one who'd made Wes feel special and wanted. But there were times he didn't understand her way of thinking.

"Are you talking about the articles you've been seeing in the papers about my dates?" he asked. "Mother, those women have nothing to do with my personal feelings. They're just a part of my job. It's only business. That's all."

She rolled her eyes until they landed accusingly on her husband. "I've heard that line a thousand times," she said with a heavy dose of sarcasm, then took a long drink from her champagne glass.

No doubt, Wes thought, his gaze straying over to

his father. Over the years Gerald had probably given his wife endless excuses and lies to cover his deceitful tracks. And now, God help his family, Ben wanted to uncover all of them.

"It's not a line with me," he insisted. "It's the truth."

She turned her gaze back to Wes. "If you say so. I just don't want you making the same mistake of marrying in haste."

Wes frowned. "What are you talking about? I hardly have marriage on my mind."

He followed the incline of his mother's head to see Vivian standing with Ella and another young woman he didn't recognize.

"Mother, Vivian is just a friend. We work together—that's the sum of things between us."

Shaking her head, she said, "I wasn't born yesterday, Wes. I can see the signs—the way you two look at each other. You need to be cautious and take things slowly, son. Please take my advice."

Wes was only half listening to his mother now. His attention was back on Vivian and the way she and her newfound friends were talking intently. Were they discussing him?

"I promise not to do anything rash, Mother. Now if you'll excuse me, I need to get back to my date."

As he walked away, he could feel his mother's eyes boring into his back. Poor woman, Wes thought. She might still look youthful for her age, but her mind was obviously slipping. Why else would she possibly connect Wes and Vivian in a matrimonial way? It was ridiculous.

Why don't you survey the condition of your own mind, Wes? Right in the middle of the wedding cere-

mony, you were picturing yourself slipping a wedding ring on Vivian's finger. That was worse than ridiculous.

Skirting the edge of dancers circling the enormous ballroom floor, Wes made his way over to Vivian. As he neared the three women, the loudness of the live band drowned out their conversation. But it was clear to Wes that whatever they'd been discussing was immediately dropped when he came to stand at Vivian's side.

"Wes, I'm glad you joined us," Ella spoke up. "I don't think you've met Lucie, have you?"

He could feel Vivian watching him closely.

"No. I don't believe I've had the pleasure," he said.

"This is Lucie Fortune Chesterfield. She—"

"Helped Ben locate our half brother." He finished his sister-in-law's sentence, then thrust his hand toward the Londoner. "Nice to meet you, Lucie. I hope your stay in Austin is a pleasant one."

"Thank you. I'm having a great time." Smiling, she studied him keenly. "You look exactly like Ben. It's uncanny."

Wes said, "Yes, but most everyone will tell you that the two of us are not that much alike. Now if you ladies will excuse us, I think it's time I took Vivian for a whirl around the dance floor."

Plucking the champagne glass from Vivian's hand, he placed it on the tray of a passing waiter, then wasted no time in leading her to a vacant space on the dance floor.

As he pulled her into the close circle of his arms, he could feel her body determined to keep a respectable breathing space between them. Wes didn't try to urge her closer. But he damn well wanted to. And the realization rattled him.

"That was rather abrupt, the way you left Ella and her friend, don't you think?"

"This is one of my favorite songs," he lied. "I wanted to dance to it before it ended."

"Considering I've never heard the song, maybe you can tell me the name of it," she suggested.

Sometimes Wes forgot just how clever Vivian could be. "I never was good with names."

"You didn't have any problem remembering Lucie's."

The hand on her shoulder slipped downward until it was lying flat against her bare back. The softness of her skin beneath his palm was all it took to yank his senses in all directions. All these years he'd never stopped to wonder what was beneath her modest clothing. But today he was seeing and feeling for himself, and the sensation was a heady one.

"I have good reason to remember her name. What were you three talking about, anyway?"

"The wedding. Girl things," she hedged.

"And men?"

She frowned. "Not you. If that's what you mean."

Arching a brow at her, he waited for her to continue.

With a tiny groan of reluctance, she relented, "Okay. They were telling me about Keaton Whitfield. Your half brother."

Wes's jaw tightened. "They shouldn't have mentioned any of that. Not today. Not to you."

She looked apologetic. "I'm sorry, Wes. The women started talking and I had no choice but to listen or rudely walk away."

A pent-up breath slipped out of him. "Forget it. Sooner or later, everyone is going to hear about Keaton anyway."

Clearly confused, she said, "You make it sound like he's not exactly a welcome member of the family."

Needing to feel her body next to his, he instinctively drew her closer.

"Welcome," he repeated ruefully. "Is that how siblings should react to their father's illegitimate son? Tell me, because I don't know."

"Illegitimate? Are you sure?"

A curt laugh escaped him. "Well, since he was born about the same time as Ben and me, it's obvious his mother wasn't married to our father. And to make matters worse, there might be other children we've yet to learn about."

"You mean Keaton Whitfield has siblings?"

"I mean children from other women," he said flatly.

"Oh, my."

The two murmured words connected his gaze with hers, and Wes was relieved to find nothing judgmental in the hazel depths, or any sign that she considered his revelation a juicy morsel of gossip to be whispered about the workplace. No, all he could see was concern and empathy.

"Yeah," he said under his breath. "Oh, my."

She gently squeezed his hand, and the unexpected gesture made him realize she understood part of his mixed feelings, at least. It was also waking up something inside him that felt a whole lot like desire.

He was trying to figure out how this sudden attraction for Vivian had started when her feet suddenly came to a stop.

"Uh, Wes, the music has ended," she said softly. "We should probably get off the dance floor before we cause a traffic jam."

With a shake of his head, he said, "Let's wait for the next song."

And the next. And the next one after that, Wes

thought. And even then Wes wasn't sure that would be enough time to satisfy his growing need to hold her in his arms.

Chapter Six

"I'm sorry, Vivian, for sounding so short a few minutes ago," he said moments later as he guided her among the throng of dancing couples. "It's just that, outside my family, I've never talked about Keaton Robinson, or Whitfield, or whatever the hell his name is, to anyone. It feels—well, pretty damn awkward."

A wan smile touched her lips. "There's no need for you to apologize, Wes. That's your private family business. It has nothing to do with me."

But it did, Wes thought. He didn't want Vivian, of all people, thinking badly of his family. He wanted her to be proud of him. Proud that she worked for Robinson Tech.

When he didn't reply, she went on, "Have you met your half brother?"

He frowned. "No. Ben met him over in London, where Keaton lives. You see, up until a few months ago, we had no idea he existed."

"How did you learn about him?" Vivian asked. "Ella said something about Lucie helping Ben find the man. How does she fit into the picture?"

He let out a long sigh. "It's a complicated story, Viv. You see, our younger sister Rachel—the tall, pretty one you met before the ceremony—she suspected something didn't ring true with our father. I don't know what made her suspicious, but anyway, one day when no one was around to notice, she searched through some of Dad's things. Sure enough, she found a driver's license with a much younger picture of Dad on it and the name Jerome Fortune."

"He might have had the license made for a prank or something. It doesn't necessarily mean that was once his identity."

"You're right. But there was more than the license. Rachel discovered several pieces of old correspondence with the same name."

Amazement dawned across her features. "Jerome Fortune? I see the connection to Lucie now. That must have been a stunner for all of you."

"It was stunning all right," he said grimly. "Since then Ben's been possessed with finding out what it all means and why our father would assume an alias."

"Why not just ask your father for the truth? Wouldn't that be the simplest way to find out?"

Wes let out a low, caustic laugh. "Gerald, 'fess up? Are you kidding? His lips are clamped tighter than a pair of vise grips. He refuses to talk about any of it. In fact, he and Ben have been at such odds over the whole issue that I'm surprised Dad even showed up today. He probably decided staying away would create even more gossip."

"How very strange," she murmured thoughtfully,

her gaze straying across the room to Gerald Robinson standing with a group of businessmen. "So Ben's search for your father's background is the reason Keaton's existence was uncovered?"

"Keaton and possibly others," Wes said with a grimace. "To be frank, most of us siblings wish Ben would forget the whole thing. If more offspring are discovered, it will hurt our mother even more."

She nodded ruefully. "That's understandable. So why is Ben so intent on unearthing this information? It's not like you need the Fortune name attached to yours. You Robinsons are already famous in your own right."

Wes sighed. "It's not fame or money with Ben. It's the truth he's after—why our father changed his identity. But as far as I'm concerned, the truth is sometimes better left buried."

As they glided together to the beat of the music, her gaze made a slow survey of his face, and Wes wondered if she was feeling the same sort of hot, sweet awareness that was building in him. He didn't know what was happening, but something about being in her arms was creating an upheaval inside him. She was filling him with desire, and things were coming out of his mouth that normally he would keep carefully locked away.

"Well, at least your parents are still married. Mine have been divorced since I was in junior high school," she said, her voice full of regret. "My sister believes they parted because our father had a roaming eye. But I'm convinced their marriage ended because they had nothing in common. They spent very little time together, and whenever they did, they were both bored out of their minds or squabbling over something silly."

Her revelation had Wes studying the lovely angles and curves of her face. When she'd first come to him with the idea for My Perfect Match, he'd figured the app was merely a product of her fertile imagination. Now he could see the purpose behind the project held a far deeper meaning for her. Because of her parents' divorce, she truly believed passion had nothing to do with a lasting relationship.

"You believe your parents had nothing in common? Believe me, Viv, I've often wondered what drew my parents together in the first place. And I damn well wonder what keeps them together. Their marriage is a disastrous sham. Mother puts up a front and pretends she's happy. But deep down, she has to be hurting over Dad's philandering." He shook his head. "I'm happy for Ben and I wish him and Ella a long and loving marriage. But as for myself, I don't want any part of that."

As soon as his words died away, he expected Vivian to fire a retort back at him. Like how jaded he sounded. Or how he shouldn't allow his father's mistakes to mar his chance for love and happiness. But she didn't say any of that. Instead, she turned a pensive gaze on the couples swirling around them.

The sea of red dresses moving to the music suddenly faded to a blur as Wes's gaze settled on the sweet, tempting curve of her lips. He was aching to taste her mouth. Aching to lose himself in her kiss.

His head leaned toward hers, and a sense of triumph rippled through him as she rested her soft cheek against his.

"I agree. Being married to the wrong person is a tragic situation. It's a mistake I definitely don't want to make."

She pulled her head back just enough to look at him, and Wes very nearly forgot they were in a crowded reception hall with hundreds of couples dancing, laugh-

ing and sipping champagne. Her lips were only a scant
space away from his, and suddenly he was fighting a
war with himself. All he wanted was to capture her lips
beneath his and kiss her until they were both breathless
and hungry for more.

"You won't make that mistake," he murmured, "if
you stay away from marriage."

"That's true. But I still believe marriage can be a
beautiful thing when two people are perfectly matched
and compatible."

A beautiful thing. Yes, carrying Vivian to a quiet,
private place, slipping the red dress off her shoulders
and making hot, sweet love to her—that would be
beautiful—but crazy and dangerous!

The serious direction of his thoughts was enough
to snap Wes out of his dreamy haze, and he quickly
stepped back from the tempting warmth of her body.
"It's getting warm in here, and I'm getting dry," he said
in a husky rush. "Let's go find something to drink."

Not long after they left the dance floor, Wes made
their excuses to leave the reception. Seeing the party
wasn't anywhere near ending, Vivian was surprised that
he was ready to leave his brother's wedding celebration.
As he drove to her apartment, she continued to wonder
what had come over him. It was as if a switch had been
flipped inside him. One minute, they'd been talking and
dancing, their bodies snug as they moved to the music.
Then, all of a sudden, he'd stopped in the middle of the
song and practically jerked her off the dance floor. In
the matter of a few seconds, he'd gone from warm and
personable to cold and distant.

She'd tried to think of something she might have said
or done to cause the change in him, but it was beyond

her. Now, as she glanced at his moody profile, she decided it was probably a good thing he'd called an end to their time together. For a while, she'd been enjoying his company far too much. His distant behavior hurt, but it was a good reminder that, for him, today was all pretend. And now the pretense was over.

By the time he parked in the driveway, the sky was growing dark, and a brisk north wind was sweeping across the tiny yard in front of her ground-level apartment. A hollow feeling was creeping over her, but she fought to push it away.

Unfastening her seatbelt, she said, "It's gotten colder outside. There's no need for you to see me in."

He cut her a wry glance. "I don't think I'll die of hypothermia if I walk you to your door."

"All right." Since her cape was already fastened around her shoulders, she grabbed up her handbag and let herself out of the car before he had a chance to skirt the hood and do it for her.

He didn't take her arm on the short walk to the porch. Instead, he kept at least a foot of space between them as he walked by her side. Once they reached the steps, he said in a stiff voice, "Thank you for accompanying me today, Vivian. You've been a good sport about it all."

A good sport. A work buddy. That's all you'll ever be to Wes Robinson.

The mocking voice in Vivian's head was hurtful. Because it was speaking the truth. And that was something she desperately needed to face and accept.

Swallowing the thickness in her throat, she said, "You're welcome, Wes. Thank you for inviting me. The wedding was a fairy tale, and so was the reception. It's been a memorable day for me."

Frown lines appeared in the middle of his forehead

and she suddenly realized he was peering at something over her shoulder. Turning, she spotted a box lying at the foot of the storm door.

"Oh! I wasn't expecting a delivery."

"Maybe you'd better see what it is," Wes suggested. "Someone could be pulling a prank."

She chuckled. "This isn't Halloween, Wes. It's Valentine's Day."

"I'm sure you've broken a heart or two in the past."

"Sure. I'm a femme fatale," she joked.

Vivian collected the box from the concrete floor and quickly pulled off the lid. To her surprise, she found a beautiful bouquet of dark pink roses and a small card with a brief message.

"Looks like you have an admirer," Wes commented.

For one split second before she'd found the card, Vivian had foolishly imagined Wes had sent the flowers as a Valentine's gift. A way to thank her for being his date. She should have known better. Wes didn't send flowers to women who worked for him. He saved that sort of thing for his real dates.

"Roses from one of the My Perfect Match dates," she told him. "How nice of him to remember me on Valentine's Day."

For the first time since the two of them had been dancing together, a genuine smile crossed his face.

"Must be a thoughtful guy. Are you going to see him again?"

She placed the lid back on the boxed flowers and balanced them beneath one arm while she unlocked the entrance to her apartment. Once she had the door open, she turned awkwardly back to him.

"Perhaps. But I'm not about to limit myself. The app went on sale today, so hopefully the pool of bachelors should grow from the small test group. I'm anxious to see what else the computer picks for me."

"I've got to admit, Viv, that so far I'm impressed with the app. I've had some great dates, and it appears that you have, too. Maybe we'll both come out winners in this dating game."

A game. Vivian inwardly sighed. She supposed he would consider the whole matter a contest between them. He wasn't in the market for a serious relationship, and considering the way he felt about his father, she doubted that would ever change.

"I suppose both of us will win if the app is a success," she said simply.

"I couldn't have said it better," he agreed, then leaned over and pressed a chaste kiss to her cold cheek. "Happy Valentine's Day."

Resisting the urge to touch the spot he'd just kissed, she murmured, "Happy Valentine's Day to you, too."

"Thanks. See you Monday. At the office."

He turned to step off the porch, and the sight of his retreating back sent a pang of loss rushing through her. Before she realized what she was about to do, she said, "Uh—Wes, would you like to come in for coffee? The evening is still early."

Pausing, he glanced at his watch as though to calculate whether he could spend any more time with her, and for a second she wished she could take back the invitation. He'd already whisked her away from the reception party at a ridiculously early hour. That should've been a loud and clear signal that he was more than tired of her company

"It is still early," he agreed. "And after all that champagne and punch, coffee would be nice. Thank you, Viv."

The elation rushing through her was ridiculous, and though she tried to stem it, she couldn't stop a bright smile from spreading across her face.

"Great. Let's get out of the cold."

They entered the apartment, and after she'd secured the door behind him, she gestured casually toward the couch. "Make yourself comfortable. Or if you'd rather, you can join me in the kitchen."

"I'll go with you," he said. "You probably won't believe this, but I can do a few things in the kitchen. Even make coffee."

She chuckled as he followed her through a wide doorway and into an L-shaped kitchen with a small dining area.

"I believe you can drop a little plastic cup into a machine and press a button."

"There's nothing wrong with making coffee that way."

She playfully wrinkled her nose at him. "Go ahead and have a seat. Tonight I'm letting you off coffee detail."

She dropped the box of roses onto the tabletop and wondered why she wasn't feeling more thrilled about receiving the romantic gift. It wasn't often that she received flowers from a man. And yet the app date, who'd been attentive enough to remember her on Valentine's Day, had done nothing to make her heart flutter with eager excitement. When he'd smiled or touched her hand, she'd felt as though she was talking to a brother, cousin or friend. Not a potential lover.

Wes gestured to the box of roses. "You'd better put those in water. You wouldn't want them to wilt."

"I'll take care of them. After all, the flowers might be the only thing I get out of My Perfect Match," she said, then tried to add a lighthearted laugh, but the strained sound resembled a sob more than a chuckle.

He took a seat at the little glass dining table while Vivian removed her cape and draped it over the back of a chair. She would've liked to change out of her dress, but since he was stuck in his formal clothes, she felt it would be impolite to make herself more comfortable. Besides, after tonight, she'd probably never have another chance to wear such a fancy dress. She might as well make the most of it.

He said, "Looks to me like you're off to a good start. And we're just now getting started with our dates. You might find Mr. Wonderful out of this thing."

Strange, but right now she couldn't imagine herself falling in love with any man. Each time she tried to picture herself as a bride or a wife, Wes's face kept getting in the way. Besides not making any sense, it was downright annoying.

"And perhaps you'll find the woman who's ideal for you," she countered.

He made a scoffing noise. "You don't actually believe a person can be perfect, do you?"

"The app is named My Perfect Match, not My Perfect Person," she reasoned.

"I stand corrected."

He drummed his fingers on the tabletop, and Vivian glanced around to see him making a survey of his surroundings. No doubt her modest apartment was unlike anything he was accustomed to. And she'd bet every dollar she owned that he'd never dated a woman of her social standing. Now that he was seeing her in her domain, he was probably wondering what had possessed him to take her to a family wedding. The idea cut into her far more than it should have.

She turned back to the coffeemaker and tried to focus on her task instead of her boss.

Silence engulfed the room before he finally asked, "Do you normally go out on Valentine's Day?"

"On a date?" she asked.

"Any other way doesn't count. It's a day for being with the one you love," he said, then quickly followed that with a derisive little laugh. "At least the one you love on that particular day."

She wanted to ask him if he'd ever been in love, but after the way he'd clammed up at the wedding reception, she decided getting that personal wouldn't be a good idea. Anyway, it was none of her business if Wes had ever loved a woman. And it never would be.

She said, "I've had a few Valentine's Day dates. Some of them were nice and some were stinkers. Funny, but the awful ones are the ones I remember the most. What about you?"

With the coffee brewing, Vivian busied herself finding a vase and filling it with water. Out of the corner of her eye, she saw Wes slipping out of his jacket and loosening his tie. At least he appeared to be relaxing, she thought. The fact help ease some of the tension that had coiled her in knots the moment the two of them had entered the apartment.

"Same with me. You try to forget the bad ones, but those are the ones that stick in your mind. One year Ben talked me into going on a blind double date with him on Valentine's Day. That evening turned out to be disastrous. I thought all four of us were going to be thrown out of the nightclub or arrested."

Laughing at the absurd image, she carried the vase over to the table and placed the bunch of roses into the water. "You being rowdy? That's hard to imagine."

A wan smile curved one corner of his lips. "Anything can happen when you're out with Ben, and I knew better than to go with him in the first place. But he can be awfully persuasive when he wants to be."

She eased into the chair across from him. "I've always thought having a twin must be very different from having just a brother or sister," she said thoughtfully.

"It's a connection you can't explain. Even though we have different mindsets, we're there for each other. That's not to say we don't have our share of disagreements, because we do. But no matter what goes on in our lives, we'll always be like this." He held up crossed fingers.

"I'm surprised to hear you say that," she said. Then, as she watched one of his brows arch in question, she quickly added, "I mean, I've always had the impression that you and Ben were competitive. That must surely put a strain on your relationship."

His eyes narrowed. "Why don't you come out and say you're talking about the COO position?"

Vivian blushed, then shook her head. "I merely meant being competitive in general. But now that you've brought it up, I might as well tell you that I heard through the office grapevine that you were on the outs with your brother. Actually, I heard you were angry with him because he landed the job."

The corners of his mouth turned downward, and a part of Vivian wished she'd not said anything about Ben or the COO position. Now that she'd learned Wes could laugh and smile, she wanted to see that charming side of him, not the harried businessman who often worked himself to the point of exhaustion.

"Who's been talking that nonsense to you? Adelle?"

"Are you kidding? Adelle is your staunch supporter.

She'd never utter anything personal about you to me. No, I inadvertently overheard a conversation going on between some of the other employees."

With a frown still marring his forehead, he said, "Well, it's not true. I wasn't angry with Ben. He didn't appoint himself to the position. Our father made the decision to do that."

"I see."

"I'm not sure you do. Ben is ambitious, but that's hardly a crime. I'm driven, too. Only in a different way. I wanted that position all right, but I can survive without it. I wouldn't want to live without my twin. Understand?"

She smiled. "I do. And you know what I think about it?"

"I'm sure you're going to tell me."

"You're too good at what you do to be working in any other position than the one you're in now."

"Should I take that as a compliment?" he asked.

She laughed softly. "You'd better. It might be the only one you get out of me."

By now the little kitchen was filled with the aroma of freshly brewed coffee. Wes thoughtfully watched Vivian as she left the table and began to gather cups, cream and sugar.

"I have chocolate chip cookies if you'd like some," she offered.

"No, thanks. I'm still full of wedding cake."

"So am I," she told him. "It wasn't enough for me to eat a piece of wedding cake. I had to have a piece of the groom's cake, too."

He didn't know what had made him accept Vivian's invitation for coffee. After the wild feelings he'd been

"Wait, Trav! This is too big a decision to make without talking it over. Let's…let's use this time together to make sure it's what you really want."

"I'm sure. Now."

"Well, I'm not." Her brown eyes showed an agony of doubt. "The military's been your whole life up to now."

"Wrong." He laid his hand over hers, felt the warmth of her palm against his sternum. "You came first, Katydid. Before the uniform, before the wings, before the head rush and stomach-twisting responsibilities of being part of a crew. I let those get in the way the past few years. That won't happen again."

The doubt was still there in her eyes, swimming in a pool of indecision. He needed to back off, Travis conceded. Give her a few days to accept what was now a done deal in his mind.

"Okay," he said with a sense of rightness he hadn't felt in longer than he could remember, "we'll head up to Venice. Let Ellis's proposal percolate for a day or two."

And then, he vowed, they would conduct a virtual burning of the divorce decree before he took his wife to bed.

SPECIAL EXCERPT FROM

HARLEQUIN

SPECIAL EDITION

*All Kate Westbrook wants to do on her trip to Italy
is to get over her soon-to-be ex-husband. But then
irresistible Air Force pilot Travis shows up in Rome!
When Travis offers to whisk her off for one last
adventure, can Kate resist the man who still holds the
key to her heart?*

Read on for a sneak preview of
"I DO"...TAKE TWO!
by *Merline Lovelace*,
the first book in her new miniseries,
***THREE COINS IN THE FOUNTAIN**.*

Travis had heard the words come out of his mouth and
been as stunned as the two men he'd come to know so well
in recent weeks. Yet as soon as his brain had processed
the audio signals, he'd recognized their unshakable truth.
If trading his Air Force flight suit for one with an EAS
patch on it would win Kate back, he'd make the change
today.

"So what do you think?" he asked her. "Again, your
first no-frills, no-holds-barred gut reaction?"

"I won't lie," she admitted slowly, reluctantly. "My
head, my heart, my gut all leaped for joy."

He started for her, elation pumping through his veins.
The hand she slapped against his chest to stop him made
only a tiny dent in his fierce joy.

REQUEST YOUR FREE BOOKS!

2 FREE NOVELS PLUS 2 FREE GIFTS!

HARLEQUIN®

SPECIAL EDITION

Life, Love & Family

YES! Please send me 2 FREE Harlequin® Special Edition novels and my 2 FREE gifts (gifts are worth about $10). After receiving them, if I don't wish to receive any more books, I can return the shipping statement marked "cancel." If I don't cancel, I will receive 6 brand-new novels every month and be billed just $4.74 per book in the U.S. or $5.49 per book in Canada. That's a savings of at least 12% off the cover price! It's quite a bargain! Shipping and handling is just 50¢ per book in the U.S. and 75¢ per book in Canada.* I understand that accepting the 2 free books and gifts places me under no obligation to buy anything. I can always return a shipment and cancel at any time. Even if I never buy another book, the two free books and gifts are mine to keep forever.

235/335 HDN GH3Z

Name _____ (PLEASE PRINT) _____

Address _____ Apt. # _____

City _____ State/Prov. _____ Zip/Postal Code _____

Signature (if under 18, a parent or guardian must sign) _____

Mail to the **Reader Service:**
IN U.S.A.: P.O. Box 1867, Buffalo, NY 14240-1867
IN CANADA: P.O. Box 609, Fort Erie, Ontario L2A 5X3

Want to try two free books from another line?
Call 1-800-873-8635 or visit www.ReaderService.com.

* Terms and prices subject to change without notice. Prices do not include applicable taxes. Sales tax applicable in N.Y. Canadian residents will be charged applicable taxes. Offer not valid in Quebec. This offer is limited to one order per household. Not valid for current subscribers to Harlequin Special Edition books. All orders subject to credit approval. Credit or debit balances in a customer's account(s) may be offset by any other outstanding balance owed by or to the customer. Please allow 4 to 6 weeks for delivery. Offer available while quantities last.

Your Privacy—The Reader Service is committed to protecting your privacy. Our Privacy Policy is available online at www.ReaderService.com or upon request from the Reader Service.

We make a portion of our mailing list available to reputable third parties that offer products we believe may interest you. If you prefer that we not exchange your name with third parties, or if you wish to clarify or modify your communication preferences, please visit us at www.ReaderService.com/consumerschoice or write to us at Reader Service Preference Service, P.O. Box 9062, Buffalo, NY 14240-9062. Include your complete name and address.

HSE15

JUST CAN'T GET ENOUGH?

Join our social communities
and talk to us online.

You will have access to the latest
news on upcoming titles and special
promotions, but most importantly,
you can talk to other fans about your
favorite Harlequin reads.

Harlequin.com/Community

Facebook.com/HarlequinBooks

Twitter.com/HarlequinBooks

Pinterest.com/HarlequinBooks

HSOCIAL

YOUR READER'S SURVEY
"THANK YOU" FREE GIFTS INCLUDE:
- ▶ 2 FREE books
- ▶ 2 lovely surprise gifts

PLEASE FILL IN THE CIRCLES COMPLETELY TO RESPOND

1) What type of fiction books do you enjoy reading? (Check all that apply)
- ○ Suspense/Thrillers ○ Action/Adventure ○ Modern-day Romances
- ○ Historical Romance ○ Humour ○ Paranormal Romance

2) What attracted you most to the last fiction book you purchased on impulse?
- ○ The Title ○ The Cover ○ The Author ○ The Story

3) What is usually the greatest influencer when you <u>plan</u> to buy a book?
- ○ Advertising ○ Referral ○ Book Review

4) How often do you access the internet?
- ○ Daily ○ Weekly ○ Monthly ○ Rarely or never.

5) How many NEW paperback fiction novels have you purchased in the past 3 months?
- ○ 0 - 2 ○ 3 - 6 ○ 7 or more

YES! I have completed the Reader's Survey. Please send me the 2 FREE books and 2 FREE gifts (gifts are worth about $10) for which I qualify. I understand that I am under no obligation to purchase any books, as explained on the back of this card.

235 HDL GJ2K/335 HDL GJ2L

FIRST NAME

LAST NAME

ADDRESS

APT.#

CITY

STATE/PROV.

ZIP/POSTAL CODE

SE-216-SUR16

▼ If offer card is missing write to: Reader Service, P.O. Box 1867, Buffalo, NY 14240-1867 or visit www.ReaderService.com ▼

BUSINESS REPLY MAIL

FIRST-CLASS MAIL   PERMIT NO. 717   BUFFALO, NY

POSTAGE WILL BE PAID BY ADDRESSEE

READER SERVICE
PO BOX 1867
BUFFALO NY 14240-9952

NO POSTAGE
NECESSARY
IF MAILED
IN THE
UNITED STATES

She looked amazed. "I thought something like that only happened in the movies. Or in families with members in high political offices. Gerald must be paranoid."

"My family has always had the kind of wealth that evil people like to go after." He gestured around the neat living room. "I can't live like you do."

She laughed. "You mean, you don't want to live like this."

He shook his head. "Luxury, or the lack of it, is not what I'm talking about. Security is always an issue."

"Oh. I wasn't thinking in those terms." She smiled, then added jokingly, "But I did lock the door behind us."

She placed the remote on the coffee table, and Wes noticed she'd left the sound on mute. The notion that she might consider his company more interesting than the television swelled his ego in a way he never expected.

"I'll bet you've never visited a place like mine before."

Surprised, he frowned at her. "I'm not a snob, Viv. I have friends and acquaintances from all walks of life."

Turning toward him, she tucked her legs beneath her. "Tell me what your home looks like. Do you live there alone?"

"I live on a private estate on the northwest side of the city."

"Where all the mansions are located," she said pointedly.

"Should I apologize for that?"

Another soft laugh escaped her lips, and Wes found himself drinking in the happy sound, the vibrant twinkle in her hazel eyes and the way her teeth gleamed white against her lips.

"No. If living there makes you happy, that's what you should do."

Her features tight, she sipped her coffee, then fixed a stare on the TV screen. "Sorry. I misspoke. There is no *us*. Not in the sense they were using it."

Something was bothering her, Wes decided, but he couldn't put his finger on the problem. Could be she'd picked up on all those lustful urges he'd gotten while they were dancing, he thought, and now being alone with him made her feel awkward.

Hell, Wes, if she'd felt that uncomfortable, why did she invite you in? When it comes to women and how they think, you're totally ignorant. You're a tech geek. Don't make the mistake of trying to think like a lover boy. You're not even close to being one of those.

Annoyed at the mocking voice in his head, he handed the remote back to her. "I'm the one who's sorry, Viv," he apologized. "This is your house and your television. I had no right to turn off the sound. I just—don't like my life being made public. But that's probably hard for you to understand."

She said, "You're right. I'm not rich and famous like you are. I don't know what it's like to be in the public eye. Furthermore, I'll never know."

While she scrolled through more channels, Wes sipped his coffee and hoped the hot brew would jerk his senses back to reality. Presently, his brain seemed to be drowning in her presence, and he didn't know how to keep his sanity afloat.

"Be thankful for that, Viv. As kids, we Robinsons couldn't go anywhere in public without a bodyguard lurking nearby. Talk about putting a damper on things. It could get miserable. But Dad couldn't risk any of us being kidnapped and held for ransom. It's only been since we've gotten older that he's eased up and let us go about our lives on our own."

having on the dance floor, the last thing he needed to be doing was spending private time with the woman. But as he'd turned to leave, something about the way she'd looked standing there on the little porch had been his undoing. Now here he was once again wondering how he was going to find the self-discipline to keep his hands off her.

She placed everything on a tray and walked over to the table, where he still sat. "Let's take our coffee to the living room," she suggested. "It's much more comfortable there."

"Fine. I'll get my jacket and you lead the way."

Wes followed her out to the living room, and after tossing the tuxedo jacket over the back of a couch covered in brown suede fabric, he took a seat on an end cushion.

Vivian placed the tray on the coffee table. She joined him on the couch, then reached for the television remote.

"It's nearly time for the local evening news," she said. "Maybe we'll hear something about the app during the business segment."

Grateful for the distraction, Wes picked up one of the cups and settled back against the cushions. "Or the entertainment portion."

She rolled her eyes. "Entertainment? Is that how you view the app? Entertainment?"

"Well, that is what dating is supposed to be, isn't it?"

She opened her mouth to make some sort of retort, then appeared to change her mind. As she poured a measure of cream into her coffee, she said, "I suppose it is entertainment to you."

The screen flickered to life, and Vivian scrolled through the channels until she found a local affiliate. Wes did his best to focus on the television instead of the

woman sitting less than a foot away from him. But that was difficult to do with her delicate perfume drifting to his nostrils and the rustle of her red dress signaling every tiny move she made.

"Did you notice whether any of the media followed us to the wedding today?" she asked.

He grimaced. "I didn't notice any. But with all the people around, there was no way of knowing. Anyone with a cell phone can take photos and videos."

"Hopefully they didn't. The public expects us to be going out with people from the app."

"That's one of the reasons I invited you to attend the wedding with me. Everyone knows we're just co-workers."

He'd hardly gotten the words out of his mouth when a video shot of the wedding appeared on the screen.

"Look, Wes! There we are, heading into the church!"

She snatched up the remote and made the volume louder just in time to pick up the anchor in midsentence.

"…Robinson Tech. Austin's most eligible bachelor is off the market. As for his twin brother, Wes, everyone is wondering who the mystery woman is hanging on to his arm. Since the tech wonder boy made the announcement he'd be using the company's own dating app to find his lady love, we're all speculating if *this* is the special one. Who—"

Wes quickly plucked the remote from her hand and pressed the mute button.

Vivian gasped. "Why did you do that? That was about you! Us!"

He shot her a droll look. "That social crap is silly. The media doesn't really know what's going on, but they damn well like to put stories out there anyway."

Vivian glanced over her shoulder to see Justine buttoned up in a plum-colored coat. A designer handbag was slung over one shoulder, and a mustard-colored scarf was wrapped around her throat.

"Mmm. I'm researching information about the most popular pets across the United States and what makes people love them."

The blonde wrinkled her nose in distaste. "Sometimes I worry about you, Viv. Researching animals has nothing to do with building a computer application."

Vivian bit back a sigh and reminded herself that Justine's job was mainly one of creating commands for a computer to process. Anything more seemed to be beyond the young woman's imagination.

"Not exactly," Vivian replied. "But I can't build an application without a general sense of the subject, now can I?"

Contemplating, Justine tilted her head first one way and then the other. "I guess not. But I sure hope you're getting overtime for all this extra work you're doing. Every evening this past week, I've left you sitting here at your desk, and George tells me you've been putting in long hours."

"My Perfect Match is selling like crazy. Now is the time for other apps to follow on its coattails. So I don't have a minute to waste."

"Well, I wanted to see if you'd like to walk down the street with me to Jack and Jane's. I realize it's cold outside, but a piña colada might make us feel like we're on a warm beach. At least it's a try."

Frowning, Vivian turned her chair toward Justine. "Jack and Jane's? That's a great bar and grill, but a bit too pricey for my taste."

"True, but a girl needs to splurge once in a while,"

she said sheepishly. Then, stepping into Vivian's cubicle, she continued in a hushed voice, "Okay, I confess. I've heard the new guy stops by there in the evenings for a drink. I thought we might get a chance for a closer look at him."

The crease between Vivian's brows deepened. "New guy?"

Her voice dipping even lower, Justine said, "Come on, Vivian, I know you can be a nerd at times, but even you aren't blind or dumb. Think! The new guy. Joaquin Mendoza. He's Rachel Robinson's brother-in-law. Surely you've seen him around the building!"

Oh, yes, Vivian had heard through office gossip that Robinson Tech had hired a new business consultant from Miami. Two days ago, she'd spotted the man getting on an elevator. No doubt on his way up to a meeting with the higher echelon of the company.

"Yes, I've seen him," Vivian said curtly.

Justine was incredulous. "That's all you have to say? Every woman in the building has been swooning over the man. He's gorgeous!"

"I suppose he is nice-looking. But I have other things on my mind." Like trying to get Wes's face out of her mind. Like trying to forget how his kiss had momentarily turned her into a wanton hussy.

Justine was obviously crestfallen at Vivian's lack of enthusiasm. "Oh, I'd almost forgotten. You have your app dates to keep you occupied. So how's that going?"

"Actually, I've skipped these past few days. Work has kept me late every evening."

Justine's grin was sly. "It doesn't appear as though Mr. Robinson has let up on his dating quest. You can't pick up a paper without seeing him with some beauty

on his arm. No wonder he wants you to make all the new apps. This one has been great for him."

Her features stiff, Vivian turned back to her desk. "I've seen Wes—I mean, Mr. Robinson, leaving the building these past few nights—heading out to his dates. I hope he finds the perfect one soon."

At least that way, she could forget about him once and for all. The thought barely had enough time to whiz through her head before another one followed.

"I've changed my mind, Justine. It might be fun to go to Jack and Jane's. Give me a moment to shut my computer down after I save my work, and grab my coat and we'll be off."

"Great! Now you're thinking," Justine said happily.

Minutes later, the two women were standing at the elevator, waiting for a ride to the ground floor. In spite of the corridor being fairly empty and Justine chattering a mile a minute, Vivian sensed that someone had walked up behind them.

As she cast a glance over her shoulder, everything inside her suddenly stopped, including her breathing. Wes was standing less than five steps away, and from the looks of him, he wasn't headed home with a briefcase jammed under his arm. No, he was dressed impeccably in a dark gray suit and coral-colored tie. The bright shade was definitely a bold move for him, and Vivian could only think this must be an important date for him.

"Good evening, ladies," he greeted them, his cool blue gaze assessing both women. "Headed home for the evening?"

"Yes," Vivian blurted.

At the same time, Justine piped up, "No, we're on our way to have cocktails. Would you like to join us, Mr. Robinson?"

With strangulation on her mind, Vivian cut her friend a sharp look of warning, but it seemed to go over Justine's head as the other woman cast Wes an inviting smile.

His handsome face a stoic mask, Wes straightened the knot of his tie. "No, thanks. I'm meeting someone."

Even though his announcement came as no surprise, it still managed to cut her deep.

You're a little fool, Vivian. Just because the man gave you a few kisses, you got the idea he cared. That's laughable. Women like you are an afterthought for Wes Robinson.

Her jaw tight, her fingers curled into her palms, Vivian stared at him. "Going on one of your app dates?" she couldn't resist asking.

The smirk on his face made Vivian wish she could slap it off.

"That's right. I'm beginning to think this lady might be the one. My Perfect Match appears to be delivering exactly what you promised it would."

Was that sarcasm or sincerity she heard in his voice? Vivian couldn't decide which. Either way, it shouldn't matter to her. But it did matter. Far, far too much.

"I couldn't be happier," she said stiffly, while wondering if the elevator had gotten stuck on a higher floor. She'd never had to wait this long for the doors to open.

Oblivious to the tension between Vivian and Wes, Justine spoke up jokingly, "Hey, maybe I better try the thing. I'm getting tired of my lame dates."

Wes narrowed his eyes on Vivian. "What about you? Found Mr. Perfect yet?"

For a few seconds that night in her apartment, she'd been certain she'd found him. But that misjudgment had shown her how easily a woman could be confused in the heat of passion. After dealing with Wes's hot

and cold attitude, she could see how her mother had made the mistake of jumping into a marriage that was doomed from the start.

"I'm going on a second round tomorrow night," she said in the brightest voice she could muster. "With David—my Valentine date."

The word *Valentine* must have caught his attention, because his eyes narrowed and the corners of his mouth tightened. "Valentine?"

"Yes, you ought to remember—the rose man."

"Yes, I do remember. Vaguely."

Unable to stand another second in the man's company, Vivian grabbed Justine's arm. "Come on. Let's take the stairs. It'll be quicker."

As Vivian hurried her friend toward the stairwell, Justine nearly stumbled.

"Viv! You're acting like the fire alarm just went off. What has come over you?"

"I've been in a foggy haze, Justine. But everything has just become crystal clear. That's what." And the next time she got within ten feet of Wes Robinson, she promised herself, she was going to feel nothing. Nothing at all.

The next evening, Vivian was so busy with George on the technical routes for the new Perfect apps, she almost forgot the time.

"Oh, no!" she exclaimed as she noticed the clock in the corner of the monitor. "I have less than an hour to change clothes and be across town!"

Jumping to her feet, she started tossing her cell phone and a few more personal items into her purse. George looked up from his scribbled notes.

"Another date with Wes Robinson?"

Vivian paused. "Wes? Why in the world would you think I'd be going out with our boss?"

The big man shrugged. "I saw pictures in the paper of you two together at Ben's wedding. I assumed—"

"You assumed wrong," she cut in quickly. "That was simply business. Nothing more. I'm meeting one of my app dates."

"Oh. My mistake. I just always thought you and the boss were friendly."

"*Tolerant* is a better word. And right now we're not even that." She gestured toward the notes spread in front of him. "Why don't you put the work away and head home? We'll start again in the morning."

"Yeah. I think I will. Liz hasn't been feeling well. She wants to roam at night—looking for a boyfriend, I suppose, and the cold weather has given her a cold. Anyway, it will be time for her medicine soon."

Liz, George's black-and-white cat, was the closest thing he had to a family. Vivian had often watched the man leave from work and wondered if he ever got lonely. Vivian had once asked him why he'd never attempted to take a wife and have children. He'd told her he enjoyed his own company.

"I'll see you in the morning, George. And take good care of Liz—she can't help that she wants a man once in a while."

Vivian left the cubicle with her purse and the dress and heels she'd brought to work with her. As she headed to the nearest restroom to ready herself for her date, she wondered if George might have a good idea. Being alone was better than being miserable with the wrong person. Better yet, maybe she should forget about find-

ing the right man and simply enjoy being single and independent, like her sister Michelle.

But that wouldn't get her the children she wanted or a home filled with all the special things that having a family could give her, she mentally argued as she pulled a cream-colored sweater dress over her head, then shoved the clingy material down her hips.

She wasn't the least bit convinced that David, or Mr. Valentine, as she thought of him, was going to be that man, but she had to start somewhere. And if a date with him was enough to push Wes from her mind, then she'd consider the whole night a huge success.

With her dress and high heels on, Vivian quickly refreshed her makeup, then turned her attention to her long brown, honey-streaked hair. The rainy day had brought out the frizz, but she didn't have time to do more than flick a brush through it. But her hair was hardly a worry. David didn't place much interest in physical appearances. He was the intellectual sort who enjoyed discussing fine arts and foreign travels. And tonight she was determined not to be bored. Instead, she was going to be an attentive listener.

After one last glance in the mirror, she left the restroom and was halfway to the elevator when she suddenly remembered she'd forgotten her coat. And since the temperature was far too low to try to brave it without the garment, she had no choice but to head back to her work cubicle, where she'd left the coat hanging on the back of a chair.

For the past week, Wes had hardly lifted his head from his work, and in spite of what he'd told Vivian last night as they stood waiting on the elevator, he'd dated

a new woman every night. He certainly wasn't on the brink of finding his lifelong mate.

But then, Wes wasn't looking for love. He was simply following through with his vow to the public to use My Perfect Match. After his date last night, though, he'd decided he needed a break from wining and dining and trying to remain on his most charming behavior. Frankly, he was tired of women and tired of work.

So why are you walking straight to Vivian's work area? he asked himself. *Why aren't you leaving for home, where you can grab a tumbler of Scotch and turn on an NBA game?*

The questions going off in his head caused Wes to pause in the middle of the corridor and ponder his motives. Several days had passed since he'd worked with Vivian. He'd missed seeing her and talking with her, even about something as simple as the weather. And now that she'd started creating more of the Perfect apps, he had every right to stop by her desk and see how her work was progressing.

The idea pushed him forward, and that was when he spotted her rounding a corner. A cream-colored dress clung to her body, outlining each and every curve she possessed, while her brown hair swirled about her face like a dark cloud tipped with gold dust. And a crazy thrill of pleasure rushed through him as he watched her graceful strut carry her straight toward him.

That day at Ben's wedding, he'd believed it would be impossible for her to look any lovelier. But tonight, as he drew closer to her, he realized he'd been wrong. There was something different about her, or maybe it was something he was just now noticing. Either way, there was a sensuality about her that stole his breath away.

"Hello, Viv. Fancy running into you this evening."

"Go figure. I'm at least twenty feet from my work area. Who would ever guess I'd be hanging around this part of the building?"

"Hmm. I just happen to be the vice president of the developmental department. It's just a wild chance that I'd be on this floor."

"Okay," she conceded, then arched a brow at him. "So what's up? Adelle gone home to leave you with the dirty work of talking to me?"

His nostrils flared as his gaze roamed the familiar lines and angles of her face. "Since when did your mouth get so full of sarcasm?"

"I refuse to answer that question on the grounds it might incriminate me."

She infuriated him. So why was he having to fight to keep from grabbing her right there in the corridor and kissing her senseless? He was losing his mind. That was the only excuse for the crazy feelings that seemed to hit him out of nowhere.

"You're all dressed up this evening," he observed. "You look enchanting."

Her gaze darted away from his, and then she swallowed. Wes wondered what she was thinking. About the date she was about to meet? The notion slashed him with jealousy so strong it staggered him.

"I'm going out," she said. "With David."

His stomach clenched. "Good for you. Maybe he'll send you more roses. But right now we need to talk—in my office."

He didn't know why that last had come out of his mouth. But now that it had, he felt a weird measure of relief.

"Talk? Now? I don't have time!"

"I'm sure Mr. Valentine will wait," he said smoothly.

Then, wrapping his hand around her upper arm, he urged her down the corridor to his office.

Except for a tiny night-light glowing on Adelle's desk, the secretary's work space was quiet and dark. Wes didn't bother switching on another light. Instead, he led her straight through to his office and shut the door behind him.

A small ceiling lamp, which was always on, sent a pool of dim light over the couch. Between its glow and that of the city lights filtering through the plate glass behind his desk, it was enough to see his way.

After he'd switched on a banker's lamp situated on one corner of his desk, he turned back to Vivian. She was standing a few steps away, her back rigid, her mouth pressed into a flat line. Even in an irritated state, she excited him. Which didn't make sense at all. He'd worked closely with the woman for years and never stopped to look at her. Never felt her presence touching him, enticing him. What had happened to make everything suddenly change? he wondered wildly.

"Okay, here we are," she said in a strained voice. "What do we need to discuss? Have you decided you want me to shelve the plans for the other Perfect apps?"

"No. Quite the contrary. I'd like for you to build them as quickly as you can."

She stepped toward him, her lips parted with faint surprise. As Wes's gaze zeroed in on them, the twisted knot in his gut unfurled, then burst into a simmering fire.

"Then what? I need to go—"

Yes, she needed to go to her new man, he thought, feeling sick. And he needed to think up some legitimate reason for bringing her to his office before she guessed he was simply playing a stalling game.

Snatching at the first thing that entered his mind, he said, "I'm concerned about these new applications you're creating. If any one of them is larger than My Perfect Match, a cell phone processor can't handle the load. The phones will stall or lock up."

"I learned all about overloads in high school. George and I will keep the size of the sites as marginal as possible. Certainly within the size of Perfect Match."

Strange how the weather was very cold outside, yet the office felt like a hot, humid July night. The air around them felt so heavy, Wes was finding it hard to breathe. And each time he did manage to draw in a deep breath, it carried her scent to his nostrils.

"If the sites can only be used on phones with high megahertz, I don't have to tell you that sales will be very limited."

With a frown that was almost comical, she took another step toward him, then spluttered with disbelief. "I just told you that George and I will handle it. And if that's all you needed to caution me about, you could have sent a short email."

By now, Wes didn't care if she'd guessed this trip to his office had been spawned from jealousy. He wanted her, and he didn't care whether she knew that, either.

"Yeah, I should have sent an email. But then I wouldn't have been able to do this."

Before Wes could stop himself, he snagged a hold of her wrist and tugged her forward.

She stumbled straight into his chest, and Wes didn't waste the opportunity to wrap her in the tight circle of his arms. Immediately her head flopped backward, placing the shocked O of her lips in the perfect position to be captured by his.

The taste of her mouth was even better than he re-

membered, and his mind went blank as he moved his lips over hers and slid his hands slowly down her back until they reached the flare of her hips.

With his hands cupping her bottom, he pulled her hips tight against his aching arousal and held her firm while he continued a hungry feast of her lips.

In the back of his mind, he recognized her body was surrendering as the soft fullness of her breasts pressed flat against his chest, her head tilted to allow him better access to her lips. By the time her arms slipped around his neck and her fingers pushed into his hair, sanity had ceased to exist. He was on fire with the need to make love to her.

Desperate to be closer to the object of his desire, he lifted her off her feet, then with a half turn sat her on the edge of his desk. A groan of compliance sounded deep in her throat, and then her legs were wrapping around his waist, causing the hem of her dress to slip decadently up around her hips.

Even as his lips sought the soft skin of her throat and his hands cupped the mounds of her breasts, a slice of sanity was still trying to penetrate his overloaded brain. Vivian wasn't the type of woman to have spur-of-the-moment sex with him, or any man. And certainly not on an office desk. But his mind refused to listen to that common-sense reasoning. The only thing it could follow was the urging of her hands on his hips, the hot thrust of her tongue between his teeth.

Seconds ticked by and he continued to kiss her until he was certain he was going to explode behind the barrier of his trousers. And with a frantic groan, he finally managed to break the contact between their mouths.

"Viv! You can't—"

"I can. You can," she said between frantic gulps of air. "Now, Wes. Now!"

It didn't matter that somewhere across town an app date was waiting for him. Or that Mr. Valentine was sitting somewhere, twiddling his thumbs, waiting for Vivian to arrive. To hell with them, Wes thought. At this very moment, the only thing that mattered to him was having Vivian in his arms. Having Vivian give him every sweet inch of her luscious little body.

"Protection?" He could barely get the one word question past his gasp for oxygen.

"The pill."

With a grunt of overwhelming relief, his hands dove beneath the hem of her dress and quickly yanked her panties down her legs and over her feet. The process knocked her high heels loose and the shoes fell one by one, plopping loudly on the wooden parquet.

"Wes, oh, Wes, hurry. Don't stop now!"

Her frantic plea was like throwing diesel on an out-of-control fire. Gripped by a desire so intense he thought his body was going to combust, he freed his manhood from the fly of his trousers and quickly thrust into her.

And as her body rose to meet his, the pleasure was so enormous his legs very nearly buckled beneath him.

"Viv. Viv."

She heard him whisper her name, and after that Vivian knew nothing except the incredible sensations bombarding her from every direction. Her hips instinctively lifted to match the rhythm of his hard, driving thrusts, while his hands seemed to be everywhere. On her breasts, in her hair, over her thighs and around her ankles. She wanted him to keep touching her; she

wanted him to keep plunging into her, asking her for more and more.

She didn't know how they'd gotten to this point, or why. And she no longer cared. Wes was making wild, sweet love to her, and that was the beginning and end of everything she wanted.

Far beyond the walls of the office, she heard the faint jaunty whistle of a janitor, then the roar of a vacuum. Back inside, somewhere on the desk near her head, a clock ticked, while above them warm air rushed through the vents in the ceiling. Yet none of those sounds could compete with Wes's sharp, raspy intakes of breath or the groans in her throat that went on and on.

Everything began to spin, and then suddenly she felt his body straining over hers, felt the beat of his heart hammering against hers. She locked her hands at the middle of his back, while her legs tightened in a vise-like grip around his waist. Wherever he was taking her, she had to follow. She had to hang on and weather the wild, relentless storm whirling around inside her.

Then, just as she was certain the ecstasy of it all was going to tear her apart, his body grew rigid. As his face hovered over hers, she could see his features gripped with an intensity that transfixed her. And then as his hot seed began to pour into her, she felt a part of her lifting away. Floating, spinning, whirling until there were no walls around her or cherry wood beneath her. There was nothing but Wes holding her tight as the two of them shot through a sky of brilliant stars.

When Vivian finally returned to earth, Wes had already climbed off her, and she turned her head slightly to see he was standing a few steps away from the desk, straightening his clothing.

With her breaths still coming in rapid gulps, Vivian

scrambled to a sitting position, then slid off the desk and jerked down her dress.

Now that the contact between their bodies had ended, she felt dazed and more than a little embarrassed. Never in her life had she behaved with such reckless passion. How had it happened? How had she let it happen?

Biting back a helpless groan, she swiped the tumbled hair out of her eyes and bent to scoop up her panties and high heels.

She was hurrying toward the door when Wes's hand snaked a hold on her wrist.

"Viv, wait! Where are you going?"

She forced herself to meet his gaze and was surprised at the earnest look on his face. She'd halfway expected to find indifferent amusement twinkling in his blue eyes.

"To the restroom," she blurted.

With a flick of his wrist, he pulled her close and covered her mouth with a kiss deep enough to start another fire in the pit of her belly.

"Use my private one. And hurry. We're getting out of here."

Her head swimming, she frowned. "I don't understand."

His hands briefly cupped her jaw, then slid into her tangled hair. With his lips nuzzling her ear, he murmured, "No. I don't think you understand how much I want to make love to you again. But you will. As soon as I get you home."

Home? His home? Too shaken to think about it all now, Vivian pulled away from him. "Give me five minutes," she said hoarsely.

Later, in Wes's car, Vivian stared out the windshield at the endless taillights moving in a slow, steady stream

along the thoroughfare. But her mind wasn't on the busy flow of traffic; it was consumed with Wes and what had just happened in his office. Now, every cell in her body was wildly aware of the man sitting behind the steering wheel. Only minutes ago, he'd made reckless love to her. And now he was whisking her off to his home. What did it mean? That he was so hot for her that one time just wasn't enough? That idea was hard to swallow. Wes wouldn't have to beg or even look very far for a sex partner. So what did that make her? At this very moment, she didn't want to think about the answer to that question. Making love to Wes, under any circumstances, was too heady to resist.

"This might be a ridiculous time to bring this up, but we both had dates tonight—with other people," she said. "I was supposed to be there more than thirty minutes ago. And considering how the media is covering My Perfect Match—especially your part in it—this might look embarrassing."

"What do you mean, embarrassing? No one knows we're together. Not really together. As for our dates, we'll be at my place soon. I'll call mine and you'll call yours and we'll both give them some legitimate excuse for not showing up."

He made it all sound so easy and reasonable. Maybe that was because he'd learned how to be a cheater from an expert, his father Gerald.

"Yes, that should work." She turned her head toward the passenger window in hopes he'd miss her sigh.

He didn't.

"Okay, what's wrong?" he asked. "Do you really care that much about Mr. Valentine?"

Vexed by his cavalier attitude, she frowned at him. "No. It's just that sneaking around isn't my style."

"Would you rather disappoint me and keep your app date? Would you rather tell the whole world that our app dates are off and the two of us are on?"

They were *on* all right, Vivian thought wildly. But for how long? One night or two? She'd sworn never to let herself fall into a meaningless affair with a man. But this was Wes, and for a few minutes back there in his office, he'd shown her what real passion was all about. And now that she'd found such thrilling pleasure, she didn't want to give it up.

Reaching across the plush leather seat, she placed her hand on his forearm. "No. I'd rather be here with you."

He glanced away from the traffic long enough to flash her a promising grin. "And I'd rather be with you. It's that simple."

Simple. She wasn't naive. Everything about the two of them being together was worse than complicated. But for now, Vivian wasn't going to allow herself to worry about the future. At this very moment, with Wes looking at her as if she was the most special woman in the world, she felt like a princess in a fairy tale. And even fairy tales lasted for a little while.

Chapter Nine

Wes's home was located in the elite section of the city, where estates stretched for acres and acres, and the houses were elaborate, multistoried structures set in perfectly landscaped lawns.

Black iron gates stretched across the driveway to Wes's property. On either side, the low-hanging limbs of two massive oak trees gave Vivian the feeling she was entering a Gothic novel where a cold stone mansion was waiting to trap her.

The narrow asphalt drive wound through sloping grounds until the car was climbing a sharp incline edged by more live oaks. When the house eventually came into view, one look at the massive, two-story structure was enough to convince Vivian she was way out of her league.

By the time he'd parked inside the five-car garage, she was huddled back in the seat, chewing thoughtfully on her bottom lip.

"Viv, we're here. You can't get out of the car unless you unbuckle your seat belt."

His voice jerked her out of her deep thoughts. Without glancing his way, she began to fumble with the straps locking her into the plush seat.

"Sorry. I was—" Filled with sudden doubt, she glanced over at him. "Wes, I'm not sure I should be here."

Groaning with frustration, he reached for her and pulled her across the car seat until she was wrapped in the tight circle of his arms.

"Why shouldn't you be?"

Her nose pressed against the warmth of his neck, she murmured, "This place is—you are—"

Even though she was unable to voice her doubts to him coherently, he seemed to understand them anyway.

"Viv, I'm not royalty living in a palace. I'm just a man who happens to have money. That's all. None of that has anything to do with you and me."

Perhaps it didn't to him, but Vivian knew what it was like to stand on the floor and try to reach a hand to the top shelf of the cabinet. Without something to climb on, it never worked. And the way Vivian saw it, she didn't have anything to help her make the climb from her lowly position to his.

But then, she'd been aware of the differences between them long before she'd agreed to come here to his home. It was far too late to get cold feet now.

"You're right, Wes. None of it matters."

He planted a thorough kiss on her lips, then helped her out of the car.

They entered the house through a side door, and Vivian found herself standing in a large kitchen equipped with modern stainless steel appliances, but decorated in a distinctly homey fashion from an earlier era.

"Let's get our calls out of the way before we head upstairs," Wes suggested.

Vivian pulled her phone from her purse. "Fine with me. I'm nearly an hour late as it is."

While she explained to her waiting date that an emergency had come up and she needed to cancel their evening together, Wes stood at the opposite end of the kitchen, doing the same with his date.

Once they both ended the brief calls, Wes walked back over to Vivian. "That was unpleasant," he confessed. "I think the lady guessed I wasn't being totally forthright about needing to break the date."

Feeling equally guilty, Vivian shook her head. "My date was hardly convinced I had an emergency to deal with. But what could I say? That I'd run off with another man?"

Chuckling now, Wes curled his arm around the back of her waist. "You have run off. We've run off together."

He urged her out of the kitchen and down a narrow hallway. When they stepped into a large family-type room, Vivian got the impression of high ceilings, rich drapes at the windows and floral wingback chairs in front of a long fireplace. The furnishings looked as if they'd been taken right off a 1940s movie set.

Amazed by it all, Vivian asked, "Did you have the place purposely decorated with this era in mind?"

He smiled. "What? Were you planning to see my home filled with chrome and glass and sterile furniture?"

His hand was wrapped tightly around hers as they moved out of the room and toward a tall curved staircase. The warmth of his fingers was so comforting and inviting that he could have led her straight into a wall of flames and she wouldn't have resisted.

"Well, you are a computer geek," she reasoned. "You're all about cyberspace and the future."

"That's at work. I'm different at home."

"Hmm. I'm beginning to see that."

"Actually, I can't take the credit for the furnishings," he said. "This is the way the place looked when I first bought it. When my mother first laid eyes on the furnishings, she gasped with disbelief. Then, when I told her I had no intention of changing them, she was horrified. But I was adamant about keeping everything the same."

"I would've never pegged you to be the homey sort."

As they started to climb the stairs, he said, "The story goes that the couple who originally built the house, the pair I told you about before, had two children. A son and a daughter. They lost the son in World War II, and they were determined to keep the house as it was when he left for Europe. Years later, when they passed the property on to their daughter, she carried on with their tradition. And I—well, it's a comfortable escape."

And he clearly had a bit of a sentimental streak in him. The fact surprised Vivian a lot and tugged on her heartstrings even more.

They both remained quiet while climbing the last of the staircase. Once they reached the stairwell, Vivian saw no point in asking where they were going. It was obvious he was taking her straight to his bedroom.

After traveling several more feet down another narrow hallway, he opened a wide door. She followed him over the threshold, into a room illuminated only by a tiny night lamp near the head of the bed.

Vivian barely had a glimpse of a four-poster covered

in a dark green-and-gold-patterned spread, a tall armoire and matching chest, before his hands caught her waist to pull her backward and into his arms.

Bending his head, he whispered against her ear, "Finally. I have you alone—exactly where I want you."

Goose bumps raced over her skin as his teeth nibbled at her earlobe. "We were just together. On your desk. Or have you forgotten?"

His low, sexy chuckle fanned the side of her face. "I won't be forgetting that anytime soon."

He began to bunch the lower part of her dress in his hands, and her breath caught in her throat as the fabric slowly inched upward until it was gathered around her waist. Then one hand slipped between her thighs, and his finger stroked the aching flesh covered by the silky fabric of her panties.

"Wes. Oh, I didn't know I could want you this much! Not —so soon! We were just together in your office."

Her voice was so thick with desire it sounded strange to her own ears, but Wes didn't seem to notice. He was too busy stroking her, teasing her to the point of torturous pleasure.

"You're going to feel a whole lot more, my sweet Viv. I'm going to make sure of that. This time is going to be slow and special. So—very—special."

With each syllable, he moved her backward, until her legs were pressed against the side of the bed. Once there, he wasted no time in pulling her dress over her head. Then, slowly and purposely, he removed her undergarments.

As he placed the bundle of clothing into a chair near the foot of the bed, it dawned on Vivian that she'd never been so completely naked in front of any man before.

A month ago, the idea that she'd be standing without a stitch of clothing in the middle of Wes's bedroom would have been nothing more than a far-fetched fantasy. A laughable one, at that. And yet tonight, she was amazed at how right and natural it felt for his gaze to devour the sight of her.

Standing in front of her, he weighed her breasts in his palms, then skimmed his hands downward over the curve of her hips. "I didn't expect you to be this gorgeous, Viv. All those years—I never dreamed your skin would be so soft—your lips would taste so good. So good."

As though saying the words intensified his thirst, he bent his head and captured her mouth with his.

Vivian emitted a helpless groan as every bone in her body melted. Each muscle quivered weakly as she succumbed to the wild magic his kiss was wielding over her.

Longing to experience his bare skin, she tugged the tails of his shirt from the waistband of his trousers and thrust her hands beneath the finely woven cotton. The fiery heat of his flesh seared her fingers as she traced the tips over his flat stomach and up and down the faint bumps of his ribs.

The more her hands roamed over his torso, the more she could feel him leaning into her, deepening the kiss until the need for air was causing her head to spin at an even dizzier rate.

Finally, his lips gave hers a reprieve, and as she gulped in long breaths, her fingers went to work on the buttons of his shirt.

"I think it's time I make this fair play and get you out of your clothing, too," she whispered.

* * *

Wes stood motionless as Vivian slowly undressed him. Starting with his shirt and tie, she traveled on to his belt, trousers and finally his shoes. Once she'd tossed the black wingtips over to join her discarded high heels, she straightened and reached for the band on his navy-blue boxers. By then his insides were already simmering and his arousal achingly apparent.

With her hand outside the thin fabric, she touched him there, moving her fingertips against his hard shaft in a caress that sent agonizing pleasure rifling through his loins.

"Viv!" he choked out her name. "This is—more than I can take!"

Brushing her hands aside, he quickly removed the last piece of clothing. Then, with his hands at her waist, he lifted her onto the high four-poster and followed after her.

As soon he stretched out next to her, she rolled toward him and curled her arm around his waist. He immediately shifted onto his side so that they were lying face to face and his free hand could access the curve of her hip.

"This isn't right," she murmured as she planted a series of kisses across his chest.

Wes dug his fingers into her hair and, with his nose nuzzling her forehead, combed them through the long strands. She smelled like sunshine, flowers and woman. His woman.

"What isn't right? Being in my bed? We can go to a guest room if that would make you feel more comfortable."

The soft chuckle she emitted caused her warm breath

to skitter across his skin, and Wes decided it was as seductive as the touch of her fingers.

"Whether we're in this bed or one down the hall—it doesn't matter. What isn't right is the way you're making me want you. I feel like a jezebel."

"Mmm. You feel like an angel to me."

"You better take a look at my back," she whispered. "You won't find any wings there."

"Maybe not, honey, but you can still fly me up to heaven."

Tilting her head back, she looked at him, and Wes was suddenly struck by the tenderness he spotted in the hazel depths of her eyes. He'd not expected that from her. But then, he'd not expected all this fire and passion, either. Wes realized he was just beginning to peel back the multiple layers of Vivian Blair, and so far everything he'd uncovered was a new delight.

"You're delirious," she mouthed against his lips.

"Yeah. And it's about time you cured me."

He kissed her until she was moaning deep in her throat and her hands were digging into his shoulders. Then, rolling onto his back, he pulled her on top of him.

With no hesitation, she positioned her knees on either side of his waist and slowly lowered herself over his hard arousal. Inch by inch, her soft flesh consumed him, and the pleasure surrounding him was so great it was practically unbearable.

Unable to wait, he grabbed her bottom and jerked her downward. She growled with desire and then, tossing her hair back from her face, she bent and placed her mouth on his. Instantly, Wes thrust his tongue past her lips at the same time he arched his hips and drove himself deep inside her.

Vivian began to move furiously against him, and in

a matter of seconds, Wes ceased to think. All he could do was hang on to her and wait for the fiery desire to consume him.

He had no idea if minutes or hours had passed when he felt her velvety bands tighten around him and heard her choked cries of relief. He wanted the ecstasy to continue. To go on and on. But her climax was all it took to nudge him over the edge. And before he could stop it, he was falling into a dreamy abyss.

He was still trying to gather his senses when she lifted her face from his shoulder and glanced around, as though she'd just realized where she was. Wes wasn't surprised by her reaction. He was just now recognizing the walls of his own bedroom.

"Oh. Sorry," she said. "I must be squashing you."

He anchored an arm across her back to prevent her from climbing off him. "You don't need to go anywhere," he said huskily. "I like you right here. Like this."

A gentle smile curved her lips. Then, with a sigh that was almost too poignant for him to bear, she lowered her head and pressed a kiss to his damp cheek.

Wes tucked her head in the crook of his shoulder, then stroked a hand over her hair. He'd never felt so satiated, so complete, in his life. And the realization was completely terrifying.

He'd not only broken his rule never to bring a woman home with him, but also put her in his own bed. And even worse, he wanted to keep her there.

"You know, I don't think we've eaten," she said after a moment.

"I hadn't noticed." His hand traced gentle circles upon her back. "But if you're hungry, I'll have something delivered."

That was enough to have her scooting off him and

sitting cross-legged in the middle of the bed. "Are you kidding? Surely you have something in the refrigerator to snack on!"

"Probably. I just wanted to treat you with a nice dinner."

A frown pulled her brows together. "For services rendered, I suppose."

She started to slip off the bed, but before that happened, Wes managed to catch her and tug her back to his side.

"Why would you say such an awful thing?" he asked.

Her gaze drifted to a shadowy spot on the far side of the room and, as Wes took in her solemn profile, he felt an odd pain shoot through the middle of his chest.

What the hell is wrong with you, Wes? Having sex with a woman shouldn't be making you all soppy and soft-hearted. You've never really cared what your bed partners thought about Wes Robinson, the man. It shouldn't matter to you now.

No. But damn it, it did matter to him, Wes thought grimly.

"Sorry. I shouldn't have said that." She looked at him, her expression rueful. "But you and me—there's a huge chasm between us and—"

"I'm not going to allow you to continue with that sort of nonsense. I told you earlier that my wealth, home or lifestyle has nothing to do with us. And you're not just insulting me with such a comment. You're also demeaning yourself."

She rested her head on the pillow next to his, their faces only inches apart.

"This is all new for me, Wes. I've never been like this with a man like you."

"And I've never been like this with any woman. Especially one like you. But I think we'll figure it all out.

In fact, I'm more than eager to see how we fit together. And if tonight is any indication, I'll go out on a limb and predict the fit will be perfect."

She groaned. "Please, Wes, don't say that word. Right now I don't want to think about My Perfect Match. It seems rather superfluous now."

He tossed a corner of the bedclothes over their naked bodies, then pulled her close against him. "Yes. But it's our work. And we don't want the whole thing to implode. That's why we have to be cautious about being seen together in public."

After a stretch of silence, she said, "You're right. So I suppose I should take a taxi home tonight. That way, if the media are lurking around, expecting you to meet an app date, they won't see you taking me home."

He buried his face in the side of her silky hair. "You can take a taxi to work in the morning. Tonight you're staying here with me."

She reared her head back enough to look at him. "All night?"

"All night."

"But Wes—"

He prevented the rest of her protest by pressing his lips to hers. "No arguments. Or I won't let you raid my refrigerator," he teased.

Her lips smiled against his. "And what if I tell you I like breakfast in bed?"

"Then we'll have breakfast right here. Together."

Shortly before lunch the next day, Vivian was busy at her desk when a delivery boy showed up at the entrance of her cubicle with two dozen red roses arranged in a crystal vase.

Even though she'd spent an incredible night with Wes,

and even though he'd come through with his promise of giving her breakfast in bed, she'd not expected flowers from him. And before she'd opened the small card stuck within the greenery, she'd expected to find the sender to be an app date, one whom she'd gone out with after the dating site had become available for public purchase.

But she'd guessed wrong, and now each time she glanced away from her work to the gorgeous bouquet, her heart did a little flip.

"Wow! Wow! When did you get those?"

Vivian turned away from her computer to see Justine hurrying over to the roses. No doubt her friend would be stunned if she knew Wes had actually sent the bouquet.

"A few minutes ago. Beautiful, aren't they?"

"I'll say. These aren't your cheap run-of-the-mill grocery store roses. So who's the romantic guy? One of your app dates?"

Avoiding Justine's gaze, Vivian looked down at some scribbled notes lying in front of her. "Uh—I guess you could call him that."

Being her usual nosy self, Justine plucked up the small card and read aloud, "To my perfect Valentine, W." She looked slyly over to Vivian. "W? Come on, what's his name?"

She snatched at the first thing that came to her mind. "Wayne. He—er, works in computers. Like us."

Losing interest now, Justine shoved the card back among the rose stems. "Oh. How boring. I thought you might have gotten hooked up with a doctor or lawyer or some professional like that."

"Justine, the app is all about putting two compatible people together." Oh, God, she felt like a complete fraud. But she'd promised Wes to keep their relationship under

wraps. And considering the truth would likely hurt both of them, she didn't have much choice but to follow his wishes.

"So you think this guy is The One? He's completely compatible with you?"

She nearly barked with laughter. Other than working in the field of computer technology, she and Wes had nothing in common. Unless you counted red-hot sex, she thought. And all she had to do was look at her parents' failed marriage to see that sex, no matter how glorious, was hardly the glue to hold two people together. So what did she think she was doing? Leaping headfirst into heartbreak?

You're being a woman, Vivian. A woman who wants to be held and kissed and loved.

Mentally blocking out the voice in her head, she said, "I don't know, Justine. I'm going to need some time to figure out exactly where he fits into my life."

Justine thoughtfully touched a finger to one of the rosebuds. "Hmm, well, one thing is obvious. The man has class and money."

Vivian glanced sharply at her. "What makes you say that?"

Justine gestured to the bouquet. "Not just any man could afford these."

"Believe me, Justine, I actually wish he couldn't."

Frowning with disbelief, Justine asked, "What does that mean?"

"Nothing," Vivian answered before changing the subject completely. "Is it time for lunch?"

"I'm on my way. Want to come along?"

"No, thanks. I'm going to eat with George in the break room."

Justine turned to leave, then paused to glance back

at Vivian. "Are you okay? You don't seem like yourself today."

Because she wasn't herself, Vivian thought. And after the night she'd just spent with Wes, she wasn't sure she'd ever be the same again.

Was she falling in love with the man? No! She might be infatuated. But she'd never allow herself to love a man who had nothing in common with her except sweaty bedsheets.

"I'm fine, Justine. Just a little tired. I stayed out later than usual last night."

Glancing at the roses, Justine smiled cleverly. "I see what you mean."

With a cheerful wave, her coworker departed, and Vivian let out a long sigh of relief. If this was what living with deception was like, she wasn't sure how long she could keep up the pretense.

After holding several meetings throughout the morning, Wes finally had the chance to get to work at his desk, only to be interrupted by the in-house phone.

As soon as he lifted the receiver to his ear, Adelle said, "Ben is on line three. He says it's important he talk with you."

"Thank you, Adelle. I'll take it." He punched the button on the phone. "Hey, Ben, doesn't a man have more to do on his honeymoon than call his brother? Don't tell me you're already getting bored with Ella and those Caribbean beaches."

Ben's low chuckle told Wes what he thought of that assumption. "This place is dreamy, and so is Ella. I'm not sure I ever want to come home. But for now, Ella's at the hair salon. I'm using the time to catch up on some calls. You're first on the list."

Wes pulled off his glasses and tossed them onto the desktop. "I guess I should feel flattered. If I was on my honeymoon, I don't think I'd be calling you. Or anyone, for that matter."

There was a pause before Ben said in a surprised tone, "Why, Wes, you sound like you know what it's like to be madly in love."

Lust. Love. Was there really that much difference? he wondered. His father could definitely give him the lowdown on lust, but the man clearly flunked out in the love department. And his mother? If what she felt for her husband had caused her to endure thirty-five years of hell and humiliation, then Wes wanted no part of it.

"I have a good imagination," Wes told him.

"Yeah. That's why you're so innovative. You can see things I never could."

Receiving the compliment from his twin was nice, but Wes knew it didn't come without a price. "You must be buttering me up for something. Let me have it."

Ben chuckled again. "Actually, I'm calling to ask a favor. Since Ella and I won't be home for several more days, I want you to a hold a family meeting for me."

Closing his eyes, Wes pinched the bridge of his nose. Facing his siblings with more Fortune news was not anything he relished.

"Is that really necessary?"

"Very. I think I might have located Jacqueline Fortune—our grandmother."

Grandmother! "Hell, Ben, you've not yet determined Dad is actually a Fortune!"

"Wes, do I have to show you a roadmap? Surely you can see that all the signs point in that direction. And finding Jacqueline will definitely help solve the mystery."

"And how many more of our father's offspring are you going to discover along the way?"

"There's no way I can predict. But if they're out there, we need to know about them, don't you think? And they should know about us. As far as I'm concerned, blood kin should be aware of each other."

No matter what the cost or who it hurts, Wes thought grimly. Biting back a heavy sigh, he said, "And just where do you think this Jacqueline might be located?"

"I'd rather not go into that just yet. Not until I make a few more contacts, but I expect to do that soon. Tell everyone I'll be calling in the next few days with an update."

"All right. I'll call the meeting, but I don't expect any of our siblings to appreciate showing up for this news. You can't give me more?"

"Not yet. Soon."

Wes swiped an impatient hand over his face. "Well, I should tell you that I had a visitor a few days ago. Sterling Foster came to my office."

"Kate's husband? What was he doing contacting you?"

"He actually came to see you. But since you were gone, I suppose he figured I was the closest he could get to you. He said to tell you that Kate hasn't forgotten about the meeting with Gerald—she thinks she's going to have a meeting with Dad. Ben, there's no way in hell you can make that happen."

"I'll think of some way to work it," Ben assured him. "All I have to do is get them in the same room together. It'll be like setting a keg of dynamite near an open flame and just waiting for it to combust."

"Great. Just great," Wes said cynically. "And what's left after the explosion?"

"The truth."

Wes sighed. "Somehow I expected you to say that."

"I can always count on you to read my thoughts," Ben said with amusement. Then, in a more serious tone, he asked, "Is that all Foster had to say?"

"Very nearly. He talked about his wife being gravely ill for a while. Apparently, she's not been out of the hospital long. She's planning on remaining here in Texas, at least until winter is over, and from what Foster said, she's still too weak to make engagements. So I wouldn't expect to set up a meeting anytime soon."

There was a thoughtful pause before Ben replied, "That might work to my advantage. It will give me more time to gather evidence related to our father's real identity."

To Wes's relief, the private line between Wes and Adelle began to blink. "Uh, Ben, Adelle is calling. It has to be important for her to interrupt."

"Sure. I'll be in touch," Ben told him.

"Enjoy the rest of your honeymoon."

"Don't worry, I intend to," he replied, then laughingly added, "And this is one time I don't wish you were here, little brother."

Ben ended the call, and Wes punched Adelle's line. "What's up?" he asked the moment she answered.

"Sorry to interrupt you and Ben, but your father wants to see you in his office in fifteen minutes."

Damn! The last thing Wes wanted was to face his father today. Especially after the information he'd just exchanged with Ben. How could he look the man in the eye without speculating and wondering who he really was and why he refused to be forthright with his own children?

Just pretend, Wes. The same way your mother has

pretended for the past thirty-five years that Gerald Robinson loved her.

Shaking away that dismal thought, Wes asked, "Do you know why he wants to see me?"

"I think it's something to do with My Perfect Match. I'll print up its latest sales data so you can take it with you."

"Thanks, Adelle. And once you finish with that chore, would you tell Vivian I'd like to see her in my office in about an hour?"

"Vivian? You mean you two are back on speaking terms?"

Speaking terms was a long way away from his relationship with Vivian, but Wes wasn't ready to tell Adelle, or anyone, about his growing feelings for his coworker. Mainly because he didn't know how to even describe his feelings for the woman or where they might be headed.

"We—uh, have settled our problem," Wes told her.

Instead of replying, she abruptly hung up the phone. After staring comically at the receiver, he was tossing it back on the hook when the door opened and Adelle stepped inside.

Without a word, she marched over to his desk and, before he could guess her intentions, leaned forward and planted a kiss in the middle of his forehead.

"Adelle, since when did you start having cocktails at lunch?"

She wagged a finger at him. "It isn't necessary for me to be half-intoxicated to kiss you. That's a thank-you."

"For what? Keeping you out of an old folks' home?"

She chuckled knowingly. "No. That kiss is for not being like your father."

"I don't get it. What does Dad have to do with me and Vivian?"

She cast him a clever smile before heading out of the room. "For a while there I was afraid you were growing as heartless as he is. Thank God I was wrong. Congratulations."

Chapter Ten

When Vivian arrived in Wes's office later that afternoon, he immediately locked the door and pulled her straight into his arms. After kissing her thoroughly, he pressed his cheek against her silky hair.

"I've been waiting all day for this!"

His eagerness lifted her heart, and she laughed softly as she pressed her palms against his chest and looked up at him. "Wes, we had breakfast together this morning. It's only been a few hours since we parted."

"It feels like days to me."

Rising on the tips of her toes, she planted kisses along his jawline. "Thank you for the roses. They're gorgeous."

He rubbed his nose against her cheek. "Mmm. I'm glad you liked them."

"Justine read the card and wanted to know who W was. I made up the name Wayne and told her the roses were from an app date. Afterward, I felt a little ashamed."

His warm hands roamed her back, and Vivian was amazed at the familiar flare of desire shooting through her. Even after their long sessions of lovemaking last night, her body was already craving more. The reaction was shocking and frightening at the same time. It was one thing to want a man, but she was on her way to losing all control.

"I understand you don't like deceiving your friends. But for right now, I don't see any other way of handling the situation."

Situation. Yes, Vivian supposed that was what she was to Wes. But even that knowledge wasn't enough to douse the fire his touch built in her.

"So did you call me to your office for work or just to see me?" she asked.

"I want to do more than see you. I want to carry you over to the couch and make love to you. But unfortunately, I have more meetings this afternoon—the next one in less than ten minutes—so I won't. We'll save that for tonight."

A thrill rushed through her. "Tonight? We're meeting tonight?"

"I'll come to your place."

"What about the media following you? We're supposed to be going on app dates," she reminded him.

"To hell with app dates. I'll be careful and shake any media who might be tailing me."

Another sobering thought struck her, and she pulled away from him and walked across the room to where the warm, wintery sun slanted across the polished wooden floor.

"That interview with *Hey, USA* is going to be coming up in a few days," she said. "How are we going to

handle that? I'm not sure I can sit there beside you and pretend you're just my boss."

He walked over to her and drew her back against him. "It'll be easy. I'll talk about all the great dates I've been on, and you'll chat about the wonderful men you've met. We're going to make it sound like a success, whether it is or not."

Two weeks ago, all that mattered to Vivian was that she proved the theory of My Perfect Match would work. That compatibility was the only thing a man and woman needed to bind them together. Now, she was going against everything the site stood for. Something crazy had happened to her. And yet she'd never felt so exhilarated or happy in her life.

"I wanted it to be a success," she said in a small voice. "I still do."

"And it will be, Viv. It is already. In fact, I just got back from a meeting with Dad. I was expecting him to harp on the products with sluggish sales this past quarter. Instead, he was praising my initiative on My Perfect Match. He's ecstatic over the sales, and he's expecting our exposure on *Hey, USA* to boost them even higher. I assured him we wouldn't let him down."

Surprised, she twisted around to face him. "Mr. Robinson has taken notice of My Perfect Match? I can't believe it. I mean, Robinson Tech offers all sorts of items to the consumer. The app is just a little minnow swimming among some huge fish."

"In spite of Dad's questionable personal past, everyone will admit he's a hell of a good businessman. He takes notice of everything. And he's eager for the rest of your Perfect apps to be developed."

"Oh! That means I need to be working late nights until they're finished."

"Not on your life! Your nights are going to be spent with me, not here at Robinson Tech."

The possessive note in his voice sent a rush of excitement through her. Yet at the same time, she wondered how their clandestine affair was going to play out. With her on the losing end?

Don't think about that now, Vivian. For once in your life, grab the pleasure Wes is offering you and let tomorrow worry about itself.

Heeding the words of advice going off in her head, Vivian wrapped her arms around his waist and snuggled the front of her body next to his.

"Hmm. Spending my nights with you does sound more gratifying. I think I'll follow my boss's orders," she murmured as she tilted her face up for his kiss.

"Yeah. This boss," he said just before his lips came down on hers.

The next week passed like a whirlwind for Vivian. Since she'd never had an affair with a man before, she wasn't sure if the romance had her head in a fog or if keeping the relationship a secret was the reason it seemed as though her life was spinning out of control. In either case, she was slowly starting to wonder if she'd made the worst decision of her life. Or the smartest one.

Most any woman in Austin would have jumped at the chance to have a red-hot affair with Wes. Thanks to Robinson Tech, his family was known nationwide. He had more money than most regular folks would know what to do with, plus he was about as good-looking and sexy as a man could get. And yet she couldn't help but wonder if he was the right man for her. If she took away the mind-blowing sex, what did they really have in common?

He could dine at the finest restaurants or have a per-

sonal chef if he wanted. Vivian had to make do with cooking something economical for herself or bring home a meal from a fast-food diner. He lived in a two-story mansion, while she called home a one-bedroom apartment. He could travel to far parts of the world just for the fun of it, while she had to save up just to travel down to San Antonio to watch a Spurs game. No, other than the fact that they both talked computer language, the main points of their lives were hardly compatible.

Tonight, as she moved around the small kitchen table, preparing the place settings for a meal she was planning to share with Wes, nagging doubts continued to travel through her head. Last evening she'd pushed her hair into a winter cap and donned a pair of dark glasses before taking a taxi to Wes's place. And each time he'd come to her apartment, he'd driven an old, beat-up pickup truck and worn a disguise to throw any media off his trail.

The ringing of her cell phone caused Vivian to pause, and, thinking it might be Wes, she walked over to the countertop to glance at the caller ID. Instead of Wes, the number belonged to her sister, Michelle.

With one hand still clutching several pieces of silverware, Vivian scooped up the phone and managed to swipe it before jamming it to her ear.

"Hey, sis, are you busy?"

Vivian returned to the table to finish her task. "Hi, Michelle. I'm busy, but I have a few minutes for you."

"Oh. With it being Saturday night, I expected you were probably getting ready to go out on one of your app dates."

Vivian inwardly groaned. A few days ago, the idea of keeping her relationship with Wes under wraps was a bit thrilling. Each time they'd made plans to meet,

she'd felt a little like Mata Hari. But this evening she was wondering if Wes would ever invite her out to a real dinner date; would he ever feel comfortable showing the public that she was his woman?

"Actually, I'm having someone over for dinner tonight. In fact, he'll be here in a few minutes."

"Really? I'm surprised you'd invite a stranger to your apartment."

Vivian frowned as she moved around the table, placing the last pieces of silverware on folded napkins. "What makes you think he's a stranger?"

Michelle made an impatient noise. "Well, if he's an app date, it's clear you've not known him long."

Finishing with the silverware, Vivian leaned a hip against the edge of the table. "It could be a case of love at first sight, you know."

Michelle replied with mocking laughter. "Oh, please, Vivian. You? You're the most careful, cautious and reserved person I know. You'd be the last woman on earth to come down with a quick case of lovesickness."

A flash of annoyance shot through Vivian, but then a cool breath of reality quickly followed. Michelle was right. Up until she'd developed My Perfect Match and this thing with Wes had boiled out of control, she'd approached every date as though it was an amber caution light.

"Don't worry, sissy. This guy doesn't have murder on his mind." Unless breaking a heart could be considered the same as committing homicide, she thought grimly.

"I'll sleep better tonight just knowing that much," Michelle said drily, then went on, "I was actually calling to remind you that Tuesday is Mom's birthday. I'm going to cook dinner for her, so I thought you'd want to come over. Maybe bring her a little gift. I got her a CD collection of disco music. So you might find her a book or something. You know how she likes to read."

"Disco music! For Mom?"

"That's right. She grew up during that era. I thought it might give her the urge to get out and go dancing."

Even though her sister couldn't see her, Vivian shook her head. "I thought you didn't want Mom to consider marrying again."

"Who said anything about marriage? Sometimes she seems lonely. I just want her to get out and have some fun. Not get hooked up with some dirtbag who'd ruin her life all over again. And since you brought up the *M*-word, how are you doing on finding the right man to spend the rest of your life with?"

Was Wes the right man? Or had she fallen in love with the wrong man?

She purposely evaded Michelle's question. "I can't predict that just yet," she said, then couldn't stop herself from adding, "I do have one I'm seeing exclusively for right now."

"Hmm. Well, why don't you bring this favorite man to Mom's birthday dinner? We'd love to meet him. And it would give him a chance to meet your family."

"I'll give it a thought, sis."

Michelle's suggestion stayed with Vivian all through the evening until finally, after she and Wes had finished their meal and a long round of lovemaking, she brought up the subject of her mother's birthday.

"I suppose you'll be going," he murmured.

The two of them were cuddled in the middle of her bed, and now his hand was gently stroking up and down the length of her bare arm.

"Of course. You wouldn't miss your mother's birthday celebration, would you?"

He paused for a moment before he said, "That de-

pends on the guest list. Besides, my parents are always hosting some sort of party. But I always acknowledge Mother with a card and gift."

"That's a cop-out."

"Thanks. I love being told I'm a negligent son."

She shifted in his arms so that she was facing him. "I just meant that your mother would probably choose your company over a gift."

"Yeah. You're probably right. Most of us kids are busy with our own lives now, and Dad—well, he's never showered her with attention. Not the kind a husband should show his wife."

At least Wes recognized his father's faults, Vivian thought. The encouraging sign had her touching her fingertips to his cheek. "I was wondering, Wes, if you might like to go with me Tuesday night. I'd really like to introduce you to my sister and mother."

He went quiet for so long that she knew his response wasn't going to be the one she wanted to hear.

"It's nice of you to ask, Viv, but I'm not sure it would be the right thing to do. Your family might not understand."

"I could just bring you as my boss. Since we're working closely together on the Perfect apps, it wouldn't look like anything more than a coworker relationship."

He groaned. "Viv, do you honestly think we could pull that off? Your mother and sister would have to be blind not to notice the electricity popping between us."

She sighed. "I suppose you're right. But what would be so wrong about them knowing the two of us are romantically involved? Neither one would say a word to anyone if we asked them to keep it private."

His gaze dropped from hers, and Vivian tried to ig-

nore the little pain that was slowly winding its way between her breasts.

He said, "I'm sure they wouldn't. But I—just don't think we're ready for that sort of thing just yet, Viv. You understand, don't you?"

"Sure. No problem, Wes. Let's forget it, shall we?" She smiled in an attempt to cover up the deep disappointment she was feeling. "The night is still young. We don't want to waste it all on talk, now do we?"

Gathering her close, he pressed his lips against hers. "Now you're speaking my language."

By the time Wednesday rolled around, Wes was beginning to realize that something was going on with Vivian, and whatever it was, he didn't like it. For the past three nights, she'd come up with excuses not to see him, and though he wanted to question her head-on, he didn't. After all, he didn't have a claim on her. He couldn't expect her to make her life his. Also, a part of him feared that, if he did confront her, she might just come out and end everything between them. Wes wasn't ready for that. Not by a long shot.

Maybe if he knew what he'd done or said to put her off, he might have a chance of fixing things. As it was, the only thing he could figure was that she'd decided he wasn't compatible with her.

Compatible, hell! The sex between them was perfect! What more could she want?

Think about it, Wes. The woman wants love. Marriage. Children. All the important words you've not so much as breathed to her. What do you expect from her? To be happy spending her time with you in the bedroom? Since Ben's wedding, you've not even taken her

*on a date. You've hidden her as if she was something
shameful in your life.*

Not liking the mocking voice going off in his head,
Wes reached for the phone on his desk. "Adelle, would
you kindly see if all my siblings are gathered in the
conference room?"

"Hold on and I'll check." In less than a minute, she
came back on the line. "Everyone is present. They're
waiting on you."

"Thanks, Adelle. If you need me for anything in the
next half hour, I'll be with my family."

"It's about time you showed up," Graham, the rancher
of the family, spoke up as Wes entered the room. "We
were all about to decide you'd ducked out of the building."

Except for his sisters Sophie and Olivia, who were
busy helping themselves to coffee and pastries, and Ben,
who was still on his honeymoon, his siblings were already sitting at the long conference table. Seated next to
his brother Graham was Zoe, the youngest of the family.
Next to her was Rachel, then younger brother Kieran.

Wes started to take a seat at the end of the table,
but when he noticed all eyes were on him, he decided
to stand. "Sorry. I didn't mean to keep you waiting. I
wanted to make sure everyone was here before I started.
And thanks, Rachel, for making the trip all the way
over from Horseback Hollow. I realize you're a busy
woman."

"No problem, Wes," his pretty sister replied. "Since I
feel responsible for starting all this mess, I'm certainly
not going to quit on it now."

"It seems you're the only one of us who's heard from

Ben since he and Ella left on their honeymoon," Graham said to Wes. "Is everything okay with him?"

"Lying on a sunny beach with his new bride," Kieran spoke up with a sly grin. "I'm sure everything is more than okay with our brother."

"Ben and Ella are having a great time," Wes replied. "No problem there."

"So what is our dear brother up to now?" Zoe asked. "If he says he's found another half sibling, I refuse to believe it."

"This whole thing has gone to Ben's head," Olivia commented as she and Sophie took their places at the conference table. "He's beginning to think he's Mike Hammer. Next thing we know, he'll be wearing a wrinkled trench coat and smoking unfiltered cigarettes."

The group chuckled at Olivia's observation, except for Zoe, who frowned in confusion. "Who's Mike Hammer?" she asked. "I don't understand."

Graham shot his baby sister a patient look. "A fictional PI in books and movies," he explained. "And I have to agree with Olivia. Ben is just about as brash as the famous detective."

"You got the brash part right," Kieran grumbled good-naturedly.

Deciding the comments about Ben's endeavor weren't going to improve, Wes went on with the announcement.

"I think it's safe to say Ben doesn't give a flip what we say about him or his quest to trace Dad's past tracks."

"That's right. He doesn't care about any of us. Especially Dad," Zoe spoke up. "Ben or any of you don't care how this must be affecting him."

All eyes instantly turned on Zoe, and the attention turned her cheeks a bright pink.

"Well, Dad does have feelings," she said defensively. "I see them. Even if all of you can't."

"That's because you're the only one of us kids who Dad gives a damn about," Graham said.

Everyone in the room except Zoe seconded that notion.

"Dad has feelings, all right," Wes said. "And they're all self-directed. But we're not gathered here today to argue that point. Ben has asked me to give you an update on the progress he's making. Apparently, he believes he's very close to finding the whereabouts of Jacqueline Fortune."

"And who is she supposed to be?" Zoe asked candidly.

"From what Ben believes, she would be our grandmother," Wes explained.

The group of siblings exchanged shocked glances before everyone began to talk at once. Long ago, Gerald told his children he had no parents. All during their childhood and up until now, the Robinson brood believed they had no paternal grandparents. Everyone at the table, including Wes, agreed that if Gerald had willfully deprived them of knowing their grandparents, it was a despicable thing for him to do.

Rachel finally managed to get a pertinent question heard above the din of voices. "Does Ben know exactly where this woman is living?"

All siblings looked to Wes for an answer, and he had to shake his head in response. "I asked. But Ben wouldn't go into the particulars. He wants to search out a few more contacts before he tells us anything definite. But I can assure you that he sounded very confident about finding her."

"Are we to assume this woman is alive?" Graham asked.

Wes removed his glasses and rubbed his weary eyes. Vivian was distancing herself and breaking his heart, but he also had to be the bearer of his brother's unnerving news.

"I suppose so, Graham. At least, that's the way I took it. He didn't say he'd located her grave. He said he believed he'd discovered the woman's whereabouts."

The brothers and sisters began discussing the prospect of having a real grandmother. For now, it was hard for them to wrap their minds around such an idea.

With the conversation still buzzing, Wes used the moment to step over to the coffee machine.

He was standing with his back to the group, taking a long sip of the fresh brew, when Zoe and Graham walked up behind him.

"What's wrong, Wes? You seem tired," Zoe commented.

Wes glanced over to see his youngest sister was helping herself to a cup of coffee. Bubbly and petite, Zoe was always full of life, and normally Wes enjoyed her company. But today he wasn't ready to answer questions about his personal life.

"I've had a lot of work to deal with this week," he told her.

The explanation was true enough, but who would believe it? Everyone knew he thrived on work. Yet he could hardly confess to his siblings that for once in his life, he was having trouble concentrating on his job. Doubts and questions about Vivian were consuming his thoughts.

Graham chuckled knowingly. "I think Wes has been spending way too much time with all those ladies he's

been dating. That's why he looks like he's been shoved through a wringer."

Wes grimaced at the thought. The mere idea of taking out another app date made him want to curse a blue streak. He didn't want a woman the computer matched him with. The only woman he wanted was Vivian.

"My Perfect Match has had me preoccupied," he admitted. "Not the ladies. Vivian and I have to fly to Los Angeles at the end of the week to appear on *Hey, USA* again to promote the damn thing."

Any other time he'd be excited about the trip. Spending a night with Vivian in a plush hotel would be special. But the way things were going, he wasn't sure if she'd be receptive to being in his arms for ten minutes, much less a whole night. One thing was certain, though, Wes decided. He couldn't let her continue to avoid him. Not without finding out why.

Studying her brother over the rim of her coffee cup, Zoe said slyly, "I think Wes is following in his twin's footsteps."

"How's that?" Wes asked, thinking she meant he was joining Ben with the Fortune hunt.

She cast him a clever smile. "I think you've fallen in love."

Before Wes could voice a loud protest, Graham laughed.

"Zoe, we're not all hopeless romantics like you. Wes loves his computer. Not a woman."

Later that same afternoon, Vivian was at her desk, trying to immerse herself in work on the new Perfect apps, but her thoughts kept straying to Wes. And the huge bouquet of white daisies sitting a few inches away from her left elbow wasn't helping the situation.

This morning when the flowers had arrived, she'd stared in confusion at the attached card. "She loves me? She loves me not? W."

Where did Wes come off using the word *love* with her? During all of their times together, he'd never so much as breathed the word to her or even hinted that he felt anything close to it. In fact, the only time he'd discussed the emotion was the day they'd argued about My Perfect Match and whether it would ultimately fulfill its promise. And even then he'd dismissed the word as though it was something that only happened in fairy tales.

For the past three nights, she'd come up with an excuse not to meet him at his place or her apartment. While here at work, she'd done her best to avoid running into him in the building. Today, she'd been expecting him to call her to his office and demand some sort of explanation from her. And the idea had her nerves frayed to the breaking point. She wasn't sure how she could explain her behavior. Mainly because she couldn't exactly explain it to herself.

Wes had become everything to her. That much was clear. It was also plain to see that she was caught in a one-sided love affair. One that was heading nowhere fast. The fact was ripping her apart. And yet, in spite of all that, there was a tiny part of Vivian that wanted to believe Wes might eventually love her. She understood it was stupid wishful thinking on her part. But her heart refused to let go of the notion.

"Hello, Viv."

The sound of Wes's voice interrupted the turmoil in her head, and she slowly turned to see him walking into her cubicle.

Wearing dark-rimmed glasses and a white shirt

tucked neatly into a pair of black khakis, he looked all business. But what sort of business? she wondered. Did he have the progress of the Perfect apps on his mind, or planning a night of sex with her?

"Hello," she replied, her throat thick. "What are you doing here?"

The question sounded worse than inane. He was her boss, and this was the Robinson Tech building. There could have been all sorts of legitimate reasons for his visit to her cubicle. But his sudden appearance had rattled her senses.

He walked over and stood to the left side of her desk chair. With his hand resting near the vase of daisies, he said, "I wanted to talk with you."

Her heart was hammering for him. And for everything wrong about their relationship. "Why didn't you let me know? I would've gone to your office."

"I just came from the conference room, so I didn't have far to walk."

Dropping her gaze from his, she tugged at the hem of her chocolate-colored skirt, but the fabric refused to cover her knees. "Oh. Big meeting?"

"A family thing. It didn't last long." He gestured toward the flowers. "I hope you liked the daisies."

"Thank you. They're lovely."

She looked up to see his narrow gaze was cutting a path across her face. "But you viewed them as a cop-out. Like giving a gift to my mother instead of giving her my time. Right?"

She frowned. "I didn't say that. But I'll admit I didn't understand the card."

His expression turned stoic, and Vivian realized this was more like the old Wes she'd known before My Per-

fect Match rolled onto the scene. This was the blunt, no-nonsense businessman, driven by his job rather than personal relationships. This wasn't the Wes who'd held her in his arms and given her more passion than she'd ever dreamed possible.

"The card shouldn't have confused you. You either want to spend time with me or you don't. And with all these flimsy excuses you've been giving me for the past three days, I can't help but think that you don't," he said flatly.

So the card hadn't been asking whether she loved him, Vivian thought dourly. She should've known a question like that had never entered his mind. "I've been busy. And in case it slipped your mind, one of those evenings was my mother's birthday celebration—the one you refused to go to," she added caustically.

"Your mother's little party couldn't have lasted that long. We could've met afterward. And what about the other two nights? Maybe you had app dates? Is Mr. Valentine still after you, even though you stood him up for me?"

He was making her, and everything connected to her, sound deliberately awful.

It is awful, Vivian. You knew better than to jump into bed with Wes, yet you made the leap anyway. Why are you suddenly expecting him to give you some sort of promise, a sign that you're special to him?

Sick with the hopeless feelings stirring inside her, she swung her chair so that she was facing him head-on. "I've not been out with anyone! Why? Have you?"

One of his dark brows arched in question. "No. I wanted to take you out, remember? But you turned me down."

She didn't have to be standing in front of a mirror to know fire was flashing in her eyes. "Take me out? Out? Really, Wes? Out where?"

As her voice rose, his gaze darted furtively around them as though to make sure no one had overheard her outburst. The idea rubbed the raw wounds in her heart even more.

A sheepish expression suddenly stole over his face. "Okay, you know what I mean. I wanted us to get together." Bending his head closer to hers, he added, "And you know we can't do that in public."

Truth be told, they would never get together in public, she thought sadly. Not unless it was a pretend sort of thing like their date of convenience for Ben's wedding.

Feeling more defeated than she ever had in her life, she looked blindly down at her lap. "Well, none of that matters, Wes, because I—I've been doing a lot of thinking these past few days, and I've decided that we need to slow down. This thing between us flared up so quickly that neither of us has had a chance to consider what it might do to us or the sales of My Perfect Match."

His eyes narrowed, and when he spoke his voice was low and strained. "Oh, so the app sales are more important to you than us?"

They weren't, but pride had her saying otherwise. "Of course. This is my work. It means everything to me."

His nostrils flared, and she wondered what he could possibly be thinking. Were his thoughts already moving on to some other woman sharing his bed? The idea was so unbearable, her mind slammed a door, shutting out the mere thought.

"I see. Then you've not forgotten that we'll be trav-

eling to Los Angeles in a couple of days for the *Hey, USA* show?"

"No. I've not forgotten. Adelle informed me that she's already booked our flight and made hotel reservations for us."

"Separate rooms, I'm sure," he quipped.

Her chin lifted. "Adelle is a free-spirited woman. Especially for her age. But she wouldn't expect us to be sleeping in the same room. And neither would I. If anyone happened to notice—well, you know, we can't have that, now can we?"

"Okay, Viv. I get your point. You're getting annoyed with all this sneaking around. But you've not stopped to think what you're asking of me. It's too much."

She gave him a wan smile. "You don't have a clue what I'm asking of you. And that's the whole problem, Wes."

His lips a grim line, he shot another quick glance over the walls of the work cubicle. To make sure no one overhead his next phony line, Vivian decided.

She was drumming her fingers on the desktop, waiting to hear what sort of excuse he was going to come up with, when his head suddenly bent downward. The moment his lips landed on hers, she sat frozen in place, too stunned to react.

Like the swift touch of a hot iron, his mouth seared hers, and for a split second all Vivian wanted to do was hang on to him, to pull his head closer and kiss him until both of them forgot where they were.

But before that could happen, common sense stepped in, and then it was all over as he abruptly pulled away from her. "You don't know what I'm asking of you,

Viv. So think about that kiss and perhaps you'll figure it out."

He walked out of the cubicle, and Vivian turned back to her computer screen. But instead of seeing her work, all she could see was a wall of hot tears.

Chapter Eleven

The rest of Wednesday passed in a miserable blur for Wes, and Thursday wasn't much better. Even though he'd just spent the past hour with Vivian in his office, he might as well have been working with a complete stranger. She was as cool and distant as a snowy mountaintop and just as unreachable. The invisible wall she'd erected between them was always present, barring him from carrying her to the couch and making love to her right there in his office.

Now, with their work for today concluded, Wes watched with a sick heart as she gathered her things to leave. He desperately wanted to take her in his arms and remind her how good things had been before she'd had this stubborn change of mind. He wanted to promise how wonderful it would all be again, if she'd only let him make love to her.

"I hope you've not forgotten our trip to Los Angeles tomorrow," he said.

She pulled the dark-framed eyeglasses from her face and dropped them into a pocket on her blazer. "I'll be ready."

When she didn't elaborate, he said, "We'll need to be at the airport by eight in the morning, at least. I'll send a taxi around for you. That way you won't have to leave your car in the airport parking lot. Better yet, I'll come pick you up myself."

She looked at him, her expression unyielding. "No, thank you. We'll only be gone for one night. I'll drive my own car."

Out of the blue, Adelle's voice whispered through his thoughts. *Could it be that you're feeling a little jealous? That you're not the one on a honeymoon?*

At the time, he'd scoffed at his secretary's suggestion. Him, married? And on a honeymoon? The idea was ridiculous. So why was he wishing their night in LA wasn't going to end with just one? Why was he picturing her at his side long into the future?

His intimate thoughts put a husky note in his voice when he replied, "If that's the way you want it. I'll meet you at the airport."

She squared her shoulders and lifted her chin. "Yes. We should probably go through security together."

They should go through everything together, Wes thought. Like each day of their lives. How or when he'd decided that, he didn't know. But the reality of his feelings was settling in on him, scaring him with their depth.

Rising to his feet, he skirted the desk and dared to wrap a hand over her shoulder. "Vivian," he said gently, "I hope tomorrow we can—"

When he couldn't find the right words to explain his feelings, she was quick to prompt him.

"Yes? You hope we can do what?"

Spend the rest of our lives together.

The thought stuck in his throat and refused to budge. Was he losing his mind or his heart? Had he actually fallen in love and was just now realizing it? The questions were tumbling wildly through his head when she apparently grew tired of waiting on his reply and turned away.

Wes forced himself to speak. "I was—just going to say I hope we have a safe trip."

On her way to the door, she glanced over her shoulder and frowned at him. "Why would you say that? Are you expecting trouble?"

He was already experiencing big trouble, and it was standing right in front of him. "Uh—no. But one never knows about flying."

Shaking her head, she said, "Appearing on *Hey, USA* is much riskier than stepping on an airliner. But this time I'm going to be ready for any question Ted Reynolds throws at me. What about you?"

A strange sense of resolve suddenly settled inside him. During the interview, he had to be honest with himself and everyone else. But he had no idea if Vivian would even be interested in the truth.

"I know exactly what I'm going to say. So don't act surprised when you hear it."

The next morning, as soon as the big jetliner lifted off the ground, Vivian pulled out a book and began to read, giving Wes a loud and clear message that their trip was nothing more than the business of promoting My Perfect Match.

After he'd stared absently out at the passing clouds for more than ten minutes, he had to break the silence or he was going to end up ramming his fist into the seat

in front of him. And since he doubted the male passenger would appreciate the jolt, he said to Vivian, "I can't remember the two of us ever taking a business trip together. This is a first."

She pulled off her glasses and propped the open pages of the book against her abdomen before she looked over at him. Wes felt his heart do a little flip as his gaze scanned her lovely face, downward over the pretty blue dress cinched in at her waist, and on to the pearls dangling from her ears. Had she always looked like this and he'd been too blind with work to notice? Or had she changed on the outside these past few weeks, the way he'd changed on the inside?

She said, "We never had a reason to take a business trip together."

When she'd first approached Wes with the idea to create My Perfect Match, which now seemed like eons ago, he'd never dreamed the dating app would affect his life so much. He didn't know how that little square with a red heart and silver key, the one he'd mocked and ridiculed, had managed to open his eyes to many things. Especially how he viewed love and marriage and women. During these past weeks since the app had evolved, Vivian had quickly and surely become an important part of his life. Yet with each day, each hour, he could feel her pulling away, and he didn't know what to do to stop her.

Why don't you try being forthright with her, Wes? Why don't you simply take her in your arms and tell her how important she's become to you?

For the past week, the pestering voice in Wes's head had been haunting him with those questions. Yet each time he felt the urge to follow the simple suggestion, he backed down.

Vivian wasn't stupid. Nor was she gullible. He'd already told her he was against love and promises of forever. Was she honestly going to believe he'd had a change of heart? No. She would view his words only as a way to get her into his bed. As far as he could see, he had to find some other way to show her the sincerity of his intentions. But how? And would she ever give him a second chance to do that?

"Have you ever been to LA?" he asked.

"No. I can count on one hand the times I've been out of Texas."

"That's good. I mean, this will be a good opportunity for you to see the sights. There are plenty of interesting places in the area to visit. And we'll have this afternoon free to do whatever we'd like."

Her brows lifted. "Are you offering to show me around?"

"Of course. Why wouldn't I want to show you around?"

She shrugged and glanced away from him. "I assumed you would have a bunch of meetings scheduled. What with Robinson Tech always interested in buying out other companies, I thought you'd want to make the most of this visit to LA."

"Buyouts are Dad and Ben's forte, not mine. While we're in LA, I have no plans to step foot in any tech company's offices. And the only meeting I have scheduled is the one we're doing with *Hey, USA*."

Vivian groaned. "Just the thought of getting back in front of the camera and answering Ted Reynolds's ridiculous questions gives me the shakes."

He reached over and took her hand. To his relief, she didn't pull away. "Don't think about it, Viv. Now that you have that first interview behind you, your nerves will be steadier."

"I hope you're right. I'm going to try my best not to

get brain paralysis this time. No matter how Ted Reynolds comes across, I want to do a good job stating my case for My Perfect Match."

His fingertips made lazy circles on the back of her hand, and suddenly he was remembering back to that moment at Ben's wedding when he'd imagined himself slipping a wedding ring onto Vivian's finger. Was that what she wanted from him? A long-term commitment?

You're not ready for an engagement or marriage. You're not even sure if you know what love really means. Ben has already taken a wife. But you can't compare yourself to your twin. Ben landing the COO position was proof of that. Besides, Vivian wants a man who's completely compatible with her way of life. And you're far from it.

In spite of the inner voice of warning, Wes didn't release his hold on Vivian's hand. Instead, he held on to her until the plane landed at LAX.

Later that night, as she sat across the dinner table from Wes, it was easy to see he was making an all-out blitz to convince her to spend the night in his bed. French cuisine, a bottle of expensive wine, candlelight and soft music in the background were definitely romantic. And earlier in the day, as they'd toured around the city, he couldn't have been more attentive and thoughtful.

She had to admit, at least to herself, that she'd enjoyed every minute the two of them had spent together. Even so, she understood she couldn't let her guard down and cave in to more of what he had to offer. Long before this day had arrived, she'd been telling herself that this business trip was going to remain just what it implied. Business. As much as she ached to be back in Wes's

arms and to feel his lips sending her to heights of incredible passion, she was resolved to stick to her guns.

Having an affair with a handsome, wealthy businessman was exciting and pleasurable. But having and
needing were two different things. And she needed a
man in her life who wanted more from her than just
being his sex partner.

"There's dancing in the next room," Wes said as the
two of them finished coffee and dessert. "Would you
like to take a few whirls around the dance floor?"

And have his arms wrapped tightly around her,
crushing her body close to his? No. That much temp-
tation would be too much for Vivian to bear.

She looked across the table to the soft candlelight
flickering over his rugged features and had to fight
hard to hang on to her resolve. "No, thanks. The flight
was tiring, and we've had a long day. I'd rather just go
to my room and call it a night."

Something like disappointment flickered across his
face, but it came and went so fast, Vivian couldn't be
sure. Especially when his response came out carefully
measured.

"Fine. If you're ready, I'll settle the bill."

Throughout the taxi ride back to the hotel, they exchanged only a few words between them, but Vivian
could feel the tension building around them like steam
in a hot shower. And with only a handful of inches
separating them on the seat, it would be very easy for
Vivian to reach over and touch him. But she was smart
enough to know that one touch was all it would take to
start their affair rolling again.

Maybe she should be satisfied with that, Vivian
thought as the taxi braked and swerved its way through
the heavy city traffic. Judging from the years of ro-

mantic drought she'd gone through, finding a man who could fly her over the moon was not something to toss away lightly. She might never find another guy who could make her feel the things she'd experienced with Wes. But heaven help her, she wanted more than meeting a man in secretive shadows. She wanted one who'd be proud to be seen with her. She wanted a husband and children, a family to share the rest of her life with. She was determined not to be like her mother, alone and afraid to try love again.

Even though it was a relief when the taxi finally pulled to a stop in front of the hotel, Vivian still didn't have a chance to escape Wes's company. With their rooms on the same floor and separated by only three doors, they were forced to ride the elevator together.

When the doors of the lift swished open and they stepped into the corridor, Vivian desperately wanted to sprint away from him and lock herself inside her room. But more than making her look childish, it would prove to Wes that she was having to fight to keep her distance. And she didn't want to give him that much satisfaction. He'd already taken her heart; there was no need to let him have her pride, too.

Without speaking, they walked side by side down the wide hallway, their footsteps silent on the ornately designed carpet. Every guest on this particular floor was either still out to dinner or already gone to bed, Vivian decided. No one else seemed to be around, and by the time they reached her door, it felt as if the two of them were the only ones in the whole hotel.

"It's still early," Wes said as he watched her fish an entry card from her handbag. "You could invite me in for coffee or—something."

She tried to give him a sly smile, but the longing tug-

ging at her heartstrings prevented her lips from forming the expression.

"I could," she said. "But I won't."

He stepped closer, and Vivian's breath caught in her throat. She wanted him desperately, and no doubt he knew it.

"Viv, we can't go on like this. I don't know——" He paused, shook his head and started over. "That's not exactly true. I do know one thing. That night you asked me to go to your mother's birthday get-together with you, I didn't understand just how much it meant to you. Then later on, I realized how I'd made you angry. And I'm sorry about that."

Closing her eyes to block out the image of his troubled face, she said, "Forget about it, Wes. I did really want you to go, but later…well, the whole thing made me see that we just don't belong together. No matter how wonderful the sex is."

Her eyes were still closed as she suddenly felt his hand cupping the side of her face, and then his lips were brushing against her forehead, sending shivers of delight over her skin.

"Wes," she whispered. "Don't——"

He didn't allow her to finish. Instead his lips swooped over hers, and for the next few moments the only thing she could do was kiss him with all the hungry desperation she was feeling.

Eventually, the sound of the elevator doors was quickly followed by voices. Wes instantly lifted his head and took a step back. While he glanced around at the intruders, Vivian used the moment as an opportunity to escape. She jammed the card into the door and jerked it open.

"Good night, Wes. I'll meet you down in the lobby in the morning."

He whirled back to the door just as she was shutting it, but not before she'd glimpsed the shocked look on his face.

"Viv! Open up!" he urged in a hushed voice. "We're not finished."

She tried to swallow away the aching lump in her throat. "I said good-night, Wes. And I meant it."

Expecting him to start banging on the door, she was surprised when long moments of silence stretched into more minutes. She finally decided he'd given up and gone to his own room.

The reality shouldn't have left her feeling lonely and miserable, but it did. She was cutting away all the sweet, romantic ties she had with Wes. It was the right thing to do. At least, she spent the rest of the night trying to convince herself it was right.

Wes was hardly in the mood to sit in front of a television camera and answer questions about My Perfect Match, he thought as the taxi driver steered him and Vivian toward the network broadcasting station. After tossing and turning for most of the night and fighting with himself to keep from walking down the hall and banging on Vivian's door, he felt like hell.

Never in his life had wanting a woman ever consumed or tortured him the way this thing with Vivian was. Why couldn't he simply forget her and move on? There were plenty of women who were more than willing to go out with him. And a high percentage of those women would eagerly jump into bed with him at the first invitation. Unfortunately, most of them would try every angle they could think of to get their claws into him and the Robinson wealth.

But not Vivian. No. She didn't care about his money

or his name. Dear God, his name. He wasn't even sure about that anymore, he thought grimly. Maybe he actually was a Fortune, but even if he was, he was smart enough to know that belonging to the famous family wasn't the key to winning Vivian's heart.

Is that what you want, Wes? Her heart? I thought all you wanted was her hot little body. Someone to snuggle up with for a while, then say goodbye to once you tire of her.

Tormented by his mouthy conscience, he glanced over to see she was staring thoughtfully out the car window. If she was nervous, it didn't show. In fact, she looked cool and collected. As if she'd made up her mind as to what she was going to say and was confident she'd say it right.

And that sexy coral dress draped over her curves would certainly make the male television audience sit up and take notice, he thought. Since when had she started dressing like that? After he'd gone and fallen hopelessly in love with her?

The answer to that last question shook him so deeply he didn't say another word until they were inside the television studio, being ushered to the green room.

"Are you all right, Wes? You look pale or sick, or both," Vivian told him as they sat waiting on an orange couch.

"I'm fine. Just feeling a little jet lag," he lied. "I've been going over in my mind what I plan to say."

"That's hard to do when we don't know the questions Ted Reynolds will be asking."

He heaved out a long breath. "I have a pretty good idea what the questions will be. I'll have to talk about all the beautiful dates the app has generated for me.

And you'll have to talk about the great guys you've been seeing. Think you can manage?"

Her hazel eyes were dull as she looked at him. "It'll be a snap. You see, you've taught me how easy it is to pretend."

"Viv, I—"

Before he could say more, a young woman stuck her head through the doorway and beckoned to them. "Okay, you two. It's time to take your places on the set. Follow me, please."

Wes quickly rose from the couch and reached a hand down to help Vivian to her feet. Once she was standing beside him, she said, "You were about to say something. Was it important?"

Probably the most important thing he'd ever said in his life, Wes thought ruefully, but he'd missed the chance. And now it would have to wait until Ted Reynolds attempted to skewer them in front of a national audience.

"We'll talk later," he murmured, while urging her out of the room.

Being in an actual television studio was far different than the remote telecast they'd done in Wes's office, Vivian quickly concluded. There were cameras and bright lights pointed at them from every angle, not to mention the set itself, which up until now she'd viewed only on a television screen. The bamboo furniture, accented with bright pillows and shaded with tropical plants, gave the seating area a real Hollywood flair, while behind them, a plate glass wall revealed a view of a street lined with tall palms and filled with bustling traffic.

Before the cameras started to roll, the director seated

Vivian and Wes close together on the couch. Ted Reynolds was apparently using the break between segments to stretch his legs. He was walking around the set with a coffee cup in one hand and a pompous expression on his face.

What a phony, Vivian thought as he barely nodded a greeting in their direction.

Maybe you'd better take a good look around you, Vivian. There's more than one phony on the set of this morning show. You and Wes have been doing a pretty good job of faking an image and attempting to prove to a gullible audience that My Perfect Match delivers what it promises. Now you're going one step further and pretending you've not fallen madly in love with your boss. Who's the biggest phony here?

"Three, two, one, you're on!"

The set director's shout of warning pulled Vivian out of her dismal fog, and as their host introduced them, she forced a smile on her face. She'd gone this far; she could surely fake her way through the next few minutes.

After a brief introductory chat with both of them, Ted said, "I have to admit I'm a bit shocked at how this dating app has become a huge craze across the nation. Robinson Tech must be feeling very happy right now. I certainly hope *Hey, USA* helped to push the sales."

"No doubt about that," Wes agreed. "Everyone watches your show, Ted. You've helped millions learn about My Perfect Match."

Wes's compliment put a smug expression on Ted's face. "Well, it's been great fun following this project. So tell us about your dates. The audience is anxiously waiting to hear the juicy details."

Wes and Vivian exchanged glances.

"Who would you like to go first?" Wes asked.

Smiling slyly, Ted gestured to Vivian. "Ladies first, of course."

Without naming names, Vivian related general details about the men she'd met through the app and the dates they'd been on around the city of Austin. And with a few chuckles added in, she even admitted that a few of them had turned out to be a bit boring.

She definitely wasn't having any problems spitting her words out this time, Wes decided.

"So have you two found *the* special one?" Ted asked.

"Yes," Wes quickly responded.

At the same time, Vivian blurted out, "No."

Wes glanced over to see Vivian was staring at him in wonder. Their gazes connected and remained that way until Ted's laughter finally caught their attention.

"I see you're at odds here." He gestured to Vivian a second time. "I'll start with you again, Ms. Blair. I believe your answer was no. However, I thought I detected a doubt in your voice. Could it be you've found Mr. Perfect and just don't want to admit it?" Ted asked cleverly.

Wes could feel her gaze returning to his face, but he couldn't bring himself to look at her again. Hearing her talk about the men in her life wasn't exactly pleasant. Actually, he'd never felt so empty in his life.

"Well, I answered no because—I'm not yet certain whether he's the perfect man for me. I'm still trying to make up my mind," she said cautiously. "But I'll say there is one who's at the top of my list."

"Would you like to give us the name of this lucky guy, Ms. Blair?"

"I'd rather keep that to myself, but I do have a nickname for him—Mr. Valentine."

Wes whipped his head in her direction. Was this more of her pretense, or was the man who'd sent her

roses on Valentine's Day actually beginning to steal her heart away? The impish expression on her face told him nothing except that she was adept at fooling people, especially him.

Sickened by the idea, Wes missed the last exchange between Vivian and Ted. It wasn't until the morning show host turned a question on him that he managed to mentally shake himself back to the present.

"Wes, your dates have been well documented in the papers. So the viewing audience is already aware that you've wasted no time in squiring around a bevy of beauties." Ted's grin was close to being lecherous. "I'll say one thing. If I wasn't already married, I'd be tempted to try the app myself."

The sick feeling in the pit of Wes's stomach refused to go away. "I just happened to get lucky."

"Sure," Ted drawled. "I'd like to know how you answered the computer-generated questions, but we'll leave that for next time. Since our time together is running out, I need to get straight to the point. You said you've found your special lady. Can you elaborate on her identity?"

"Not yet. Right now, the lady's name is private."

"Oh, come on, Wes," Ted goaded. "You've traveled all the way from Texas to give us this interview. Surely you don't want to waste this opportunity to reveal your new lady love."

"There are circumstances that prevent me from doing that today."

"Okay. Maybe you can answer this question. Do you see your relationship with this woman lasting far into the future? Or is she just perfect for you at this time in your life?"

Wes swallowed as emotions threatened to close his

throat. "I can assure you that through My Perfect Match, I've found the woman who will always fit me perfectly."

The conviction in Wes's voice must have taken Ted aback a bit, because his smug tone turned thoughtful. "Well, now, I think you're really serious about this. So why not come out and tell us her name?"

"Sorry. Her name is off-limits. She means too much to me to reveal her name before we have—everything settled between us."

"Oh, so it sounds like an engagement is soon coming," Ted said happily. "Another reason for *Hey, USA* to follow the trials of My Perfect Match. And we'll certainly be doing that."

Ted went on quickly to wrap up the segment, which happened to be the last one for the show. Once the cameras had quit rolling, Wes helped Vivian from the couch, hoping the two of them could exit the set before Ted could catch them. Now that he'd practically revealed his feelings to millions of viewers, he had all sorts of things he needed to say to Vivian, and he couldn't do it fast enough.

"Excuse me, Wes. Before you go, could I have a word with you?"

Glancing around to see their host walking toward them, Wes groaned under his breath. "There's no need for you to stay," he told Vivian. "I'll meet you out in the lobby."

"Fine," she said and briskly strode away from him.

Surprisingly, Ted chatted with Wes much longer than he expected, and by the time he finally excused himself, Wes was close to screaming with frustration. He practically ran off the studio set and through the empty green room. But once he reached the entrance to the

outer lobby of the building, he came to an abrupt halt and stared.

Across the wide room, Vivian was standing with a young man he recognized as a recruiter from a competing tech firm. What in hell was he doing here? Had he followed them to snoop? Maybe he'd hoped to catch Vivian alone and pry sales data from her? Or had he wanted to talk directly to her about another matter?

The sick feeling he'd been dealing with all morning intensified as he forced himself to stride across the room. Unlike Ben, he hated confrontations, but Vivian was more than his employee; she was his woman, and this man needed to know it.

"I'll have to agree it sounds like a great offer, Mr. Clemente. I've never thought of leaving Texas before, but California does have its sunshine," Vivian was saying as Wes walked up.

The young black-haired man gave her a charming smile. "Please call me Gino. And we have much more to offer than sunshine. This is a mecca for innovative technology. And with your rich imagination, you could zoom to the top. Our company does plenty of business with the film industry. Are you interested in the movies, Ms. Blair?"

Vivian glanced awkwardly over to Wes, and it was clear she wasn't comfortable with him overhearing her conversation.

"Are you, Ms. Blair?" Wes prodded.

With a nervous lick of her lips, she looked back to Gino Clemente. "I'd have to think about that before I could give you an answer."

"Surely," he said smoothly. "I do hope you'll give it careful consideration. I promise it would give your career a huge leap."

"Thank you for thinking of me, Gino. I have your number."

"I'll be looking forward to hearing from you."

He shook Vivian's hand, then walked off without bothering to acknowledge himself to Wes. Which was okay with him. As far as he was concerned, he never wanted to see the guy within two thousand miles of Vivian again.

"So you want to tell me what that was all about?"

Vivian shrugged, then glanced away as she tucked a loose strand of hair behind her ear. "I'm sure you heard enough to figure it out. Mr. Clemente was here on the behalf of World Vision Mobile. My Perfect Match has caught their attention, and they're offering me a position with them." Her gaze returned to his. "It would mean a much larger salary and a higher position than the one I hold now."

The challenging glint in her hazel eyes sent a shock wave through him. Why had it come to this point to make him realize what a gem he'd always had in Vivian? Had he taken for granted that she would always be around to work with him? Moreover, that she'd be willing to be a hidden mistress?

His throat tight, he asked, "And what did you tell him?"

"You heard."

"I only caught part of the conversation."

"I don't want to discuss this now. Not here."

She turned toward the exit, but Wes instantly wrapped his hand around her upper arm.

"Well, I do. Now. And right here."

Wes glanced around for a quiet spot in the room and noticed an atrium connected to one side of the lobby. He led her over to the plant filled room and seated her

on a wicker couch. Once he was sitting beside her, he drew her hands gently between his.

"Viv, are you unhappy at Robinson Tech?"

The dainty flare of her nostrils told him he'd not asked the right question, so he tried again.

"A few minutes ago you told Ted Reynolds that Mr. Valentine was at the top of your list. Are you really thinking he might be your special man?"

She frowned at him. "No. That was only for the camera. Remember? You said we needed to look convincing."

He let out a heavy breath. "Well, you fooled the hell out of me."

Her eyes narrowed as she continued to study his face. "And what about you? You said you had found *your* special woman. Was that just for the sake of My Perfect Match?"

Suddenly his heart was brimming over with love for this woman, and he finally understood what Ben had been trying to tell him about finding the right one.

"I have really found her," he said gently. "I just didn't want to use her name to promote a Robinson Tech product. I love her too much for that."

Her head bent forward, and a curtain of hair went with it, making it impossible for Wes to see her face.

"Then it probably would be for the best if I accept Gino's offer," she mumbled.

Wes stared numbly at the top of her head. Had he made such a mess of things that she no longer cared what he was feeling?

"Is that all you have to say?" he asked, his voice full of dismay. "That it's best you leave?"

She lifted her head, and Wes could see a cloud of

confusion in her eyes. "Do you think I want to stick around and watch you with some other woman?"

The meaning of her words smacked him like a fist to the face. "Viv! You think—" Pausing, he shook his head in disbelief. "When I said I'd found my woman, who did you think I was talking about?"

She stared at him in blank confusion, and then her lips began to tremble. "Are you saying—do you want me to believe you were talking about me?"

"You'd better believe it, Viv. Because I can't live without you. And I don't intend to try."

Her mouth fell open. "But I thought you considered this whole thing with us as a temporary thing. Especially when you wanted to keep everything secret."

He groaned ruefully. "At first that was the only way I figured we could work things. The whole world was watching, expecting us to find a special love through My Perfect Match. I didn't want to squash the chances for the app to be a success. Especially when you kept telling me how important it was to you."

She squeezed his hands tightly as a rueful groan slipped past her lips. "It was important. It still is. But not nearly as important as you are to me. Oh, Wes, I thought you were ashamed of me! I'm so—we come from such different worlds. And I —"

Releasing his hold on her hands, he wrapped his fingers around her shoulders. "Look, Viv, I understand that we're not compatible in your eyes. And I know how important that is to you. I even agree that passion in the bedroom eventually burns itself out. But my feelings for you go much deeper than that. I love you. Maybe it's too soon for you to believe that. But I'm willing to spend a lifetime proving it to you."

Tears spilled from her eyes and onto her cheeks. "I

never fully understood what passion was all about until you, Wes. You made me feel things I'd never dreamed possible. We have that special spark together. But even if the fire dies, I'll still love you, Wes. Always."

Happiness such as he'd never known soared through him, and at that moment he felt as though he could jump the moon. "And what about all that compatibility you've been worried about? You think we can find enough in common to keep us together for the next fifty years?"

Her face leaning toward his, she chuckled softly. "Let's shoot for sixty."

Closing the last bit of distance between their lips, he gave her a kiss filled with love and promises for the future. A future they would share together.

"What do you say we start those sixty years by going to the hotel and proving to each other just how compatible we really are?"

Laughing, she jumped to her feet, pulling him along with her. "I say we're wasting time."

Much later that night, after an evening of dining and dancing at a seaside resort, Wes and Vivian walked down to the beach. Standing on the wet sand, with the moon bathing them in silvery light, they watched the waves of the Pacific roll onto shore.

The salty wind carried the scent of tropical flowers growing nearby, while farther in the background, the faint sound of music drifted from a cabana. With Wes's arm curled around her waist and her cheek resting against his chest, Vivian was certain she was in heaven, or very close to it.

"When you phoned Adelle and told her we'd be staying in California for another night, did you tell her why?" she asked, her voice drowsy with contentment.

"Not exactly," he answered. "I told her we still had business to take care of before we returned to Austin. But don't start worrying that I'm still keeping secrets about our relationship. I wanted to surprise her and everyone else back home."

"Surprise them? How?"

With his hands on her shoulders, he turned her so that they were facing each other. "I was going to wait until we got back to the hotel to do this. But I've decided now, right here on the beach, is better."

"To do what?" she asked impishly. "Kiss me and tell me how beautiful I look in my new dress?"

Because she'd only expected to spend one night in Los Angeles, Vivian had packed just enough things to fill her carry-on bag. After Wes had made the decision for them to stay over, he'd taken her on a shopping spree, buying her a whole suitcase full of dresses and other clothing to wear when spring arrived in Texas.

His eyes glittering with love, he smiled at her. "I've already done that."

"A second time won't hurt."

"In a minute," he promised. "Right now, there's something else I want to do." He slipped a hand into the front pocket of his trousers and pulled out a small jewelry box. "I confess, while you were trying on dresses, I did a little shopping on my own."

She stared at the little white box while trying to guess what might be inside. "Earrings! You've already spent too much on me today, Wes." Slipping her arms around his waist, she snuggled the front of her body close to his. "I don't need gifts from you to make me happy, darling. You're all I need."

"But this is a special gift. One that goes along with those sixty years we're going to have together." He

flipped open the box and held it up for her to see. "Will you marry me, Viv?"

She gasped at the sight of a rather large diamond winking in the moonlight. "Wes! That's—it's—an engagement ring!"

The shock on her face had him chuckling softly. "That is what a man usually gives a woman when he asks her to become his wife."

"Yes. But you told me you—" She broke off as confusion and joy collided inside her, scrambling her senses. "You told me you never wanted to get married. That seeing your parents' troubled marriage had put you off the idea completely."

The wind was whipping her hair about her face, and he reached up to gently snare the wayward strands with his fingers. "That's true, Viv. For years now, I've told myself I wanted no part of having a family of my own. My parents had eight children together, but their marriage is cold and loveless. I've never understood what went wrong between them, or if it was ever right. I only knew that I didn't want that for myself. Ben told me I'd think differently if I ever found the right woman. I didn't believe him. Until I fell in love with you. Having you in my life has changed me, Viv. You've taught me there's more to what goes on between a man and a woman than red-hot sex."

Her heart overflowing with emotions, she cradled the side of his face in the palm of her hand. "And you've taught me that a man and a woman need more than simply being compatible to keep them together. Without a spark of fire, things could get pretty boring."

"They'll never get boring with us. I promise. And you do look very pretty in that dress." He kissed her thoroughly. Then, with his lips hovering close to hers,

he said, "I'm waiting for your answer. Are you going to wear my ring or not?"

"Yes! Yes, I'll marry you! But what about My Perfect Match? What about your family and friends and all the employees at Robinson Tech?"

He pulled the ring from the box and slipped it onto her finger. "When we walk back into the Robinson Tech building Monday morning, I want everyone to see we're engaged. And as for My Perfect Match, well, it did manage to bring us together. So we're proof the app delivers what it promises. A perfect match to love, honor and cherish. There's only one thing left for you to consider, Viv."

"What's that? If you're worried I'll be wanting a wedding as big as Ben's, then don't be. Any kind of ceremony will do for me."

"We're going to have a grand wedding," he promised. "But for now, you don't actually know if your name will change to Robinson or Fortune. Is that going to make a difference?"

"I'm not marrying a name, Wes. I'm marrying the man I love."

Rising on tiptoes, she closed the gap between their lips. As the kiss swirled them into an erotic cocoon, she didn't worry what the future might hold. Her future was right there in her arms.

* * * * *

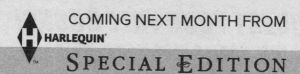

COMING NEXT MONTH FROM

HARLEQUIN®

SPECIAL EDITION

Available February 16, 2016

#2461 "I DO"...TAKE TWO!
Three Coins in the Fountain
by Merline Lovelace
On a trip to Italy, Kate Westbrook makes a wish at the Trevi Fountain—to create a future *without* her soon-to-be-ex, Travis! But Cupid has other plans for these two, and true love might just be in their future.

#2462 FORTUNE'S SECRET HUSBAND
The Fortunes of Texas: All Fortune's Children
by Karen Rose Smith
Proper Brit Lucie Fortune Chesterfield had a whirlwind teenage marriage to Chase Parker, but that was long over—or so she thought. Until her secret husband shows up at her door...with a big surprise!

#2463 BACK IN THE SADDLE
Wed in the West
by Karen Templeton
When widower Zach Talbot agrees to help Mallory Keyes find a horse for her son, he falls for the paralyzed former actress. But can the veterinarian and the beauty both give love a second chance?

#2464 A BABY AND A BETROTHAL
Crimson, Colorado
by Michelle Major
Katie Garrity is on a mission to find her perfect match—only to be surprised by her own pregnancy! When her first crush, Noah Crawford, comes back to town, will they get a chance at a love neither expected?

#2465 FROM DARE TO DUE DATE
Sugar Falls, Idaho
by Christy Jeffries
When dancer Mia Palinski has one magical night with Dr. Garrett McCormick, she winds up pregnant. Both of them aren't looking for love, but a baby changes everything. Can a single dance create a forever family?

#2466 A COWBOY IN THE KITCHEN
Hurley's Homestyle Kitchen
by Meg Maxwell
Single dad West Montgomery is doing his best to be Mr. Mom for his daughter. He's even taking cooking classes with beautiful chef Annabel Hurley. But West and his little girl might be the secret ingredient for her perfect recipe to forever.

HSECNM0216